S0-AUY-031

THE BESTSELLING SERIES
CONTINUES
WITH A BOLD NEW ADVENTURE!

" A continuously growing series of talented
young SF authors . . . These books are really
quite remarkable . . . the series promises to
be well-received by Asimov fans."
                                        —*Thrust*

"Like the movie serials of old, the publisher
has me hooked, and I'll be watching the
stands . . ."
                              —**Mark Sabljak,**
                              Milwaukee Journal

ISAAC ASIMOV'S ROBOT CITY™

ROBOTS AND ALIENS

Changeling by Stephen Leigh

A Byron Preiss Visual Publications, Inc. Book

ACE BOOKS, NEW YORK

This book is an Ace original edition, and has never been previously published.

ISAAC ASIMOV'S ROBOT CITY
ROBOTS AND ALIENS
BOOK 1: CHANGELING

An Ace Book/published by arrangement with
Byron Preiss Visual Publications, Inc.

PRINTING HISTORY
Ace edition/August 1989

ISBN: 0-441-73127-9

Ace Books are published by The Berkley Publishing Group,
200 Madison Avenue, New York, New York 10016.
The name "ACE" and the "A" logo are
trademarks belonging to Charter Communications, Inc.

PRINTED IN THE UNITED STATES OF AMERICA

10 9 8 7 6 5 4 3 2 1

To Megen and Devon
Who are already exploring their own sense of wonder
and who have given new meaning to mine

CONTENTS

ROBOTS AND ALIENS
ISAAC ASIMOV

You may have noticed (assuming that you have read my robot stories and novels) that I have not had occasion to discuss the interaction of robots and aliens. In fact, at no point anywhere in my writing has any robot met any alien. In very few of my writings have human beings met aliens, in fact.

You may wonder why that is so, and you might suspect that the answer would be, "I don't know. That's just the way I write stories, I guess." But if that is what you suspect, you are wrong. I will be glad to explain just why things are as they are.

The time is 1940 . . .

In those days, it was common to describe "Galactic Federations" in which there were many, many planets, each with its own form of intelligent life. E. E. ("Doc") Smith had started the fashion, and John W. Campbell had carried it on.

There was, however, a catch. Smith and Campbell, though wonderful people, were of northwest European extraction and they took it for granted that northwest Europeans and their descendants were the evolutionary crown and peak. Neither one was a racist in any evil sense, you understand. Both were as kind and as good as gold to everyone, but they knew they belonged to the racial aristocracy.

Well, then, when they wrote of Galactic Federations, Earthmen were the northwest Europeans of the Galaxy. There were lots of different intelligences in Smith's Galaxy but the leader was Kimball Kinnison, an Earthman (of northwest European extraction, I'm sure). There were lots of different intelligences in Campbell's Galaxy, but the leaders were Arcot, Wade, and Morey, who were Earthmen (of northwest European extraction, I'm sure).

Well, in 1940, I wrote a story called "Homo Sol", which appeared in the September 1940 issue of *Astounding Science Fiction*. I, too, had a Galactic Federation composed of innumerable different intelligences, but I had no brief for northwest Europeans. I was of East European extraction myself and my kind was being trampled into oblivion by a bunch of northwest Europeans. I was therefore not intent on making Earthmen superior. The hero of the story was from Rigel and Earthmen were definitely a bunch of second-raters.

Well, Campbell wouldn't allow it. Earthmen had to be superior to all others, no matter what. He forced me to make some changes and then made some himself, and I was frustrated. On the one hand, I wanted to write my stories without interference; on the other hand, I wanted to sell to Campbell. What to do?

I wrote a sequel to "Homo Sol", a story called "The Imaginary", in which only the aliens appeared. No Earthmen. Campbell rejected it; it appeared in the November 1942 issue of *Superscience Stories*.

Then inspiration struck. If I wrote human/alien stories, Campbell would not let me be. If I wrote alien-only stories, Campbell would reject them. So why not write human-only stories. I did. When I got around to making another serious attempt at dealing with a Galactic society, I made it an *all-human Galaxy* and Campbell had no objections at all. Mine was the first such Galaxy in science fiction history, as far as I know, and it proved phenomenally successful, for I wrote my Foundation (and related) novels on that basis.

The first such story was "Foundation" itself, which appeared in the May 1942 *Astounding Science Fiction*. Meanwhile, it had also occurred to me that I could write robot stories for Campbell. I didn't mind having Earthmen superior to robots—at least just at first. The first robot story that Campbell took was "Reason", which appeared in the April

1941 *Astounding Science Fiction*. Those stories, too, proved very popular, and presuming upon their popularity, I gradually made my robots better and wiser and more decent than human beings and Campbell continued to take them.

This continued even after Campbell's death, and now I can't think of a recent robot story in which my robot isn't far better than the human beings he must deal with. I think of "Bicentennial Man", "Robot Dreams", "Too Bad" and, most of all, I think of R. Daneel and R. Giskard in my robot novels.

But the decision I made in the heat of World War II and in my resentment of Campbell's assumption have stayed with me. My Galaxy is *still* all-human, and my robots *still* meet only humans.

This doesn't mean that (always assuming I live long enough) it's not possible I may violate this habit of mine in the future. The ending of my novel *Foundation and Earth* makes it conceivable that in the sequel I may introduce aliens and that R. Daneel will have to deal with them. That's not a promise because actually I haven't the faintest idea of what's going to happen in the sequel, but it is at least *conceivable* that aliens may intrude on my close-knit human societies.

(Naturally, I repel, with contempt, any suggestion that I don't introduce aliens into my stories because I "can't handle them." In fact, my chief reason for writing my novel *The Gods Themselves* was to prove to anyone who felt he needed the proof, that I could, too, handle aliens. No one can doubt that I proved it, but I must admit that even in *The Gods Themselves*, the aliens and the human beings didn't actually meet face-to-face.)

But let's move on. Suppose that one of my robots *did* encounter an alien intelligence. What would happen?

Problems of this sort have occurred to me now and then but I never felt moved to make one the basis of a story.

Consider— How would a robot define a human being in the light of the three laws. The First Law, it seems to me, offers no difficulty: "A robot may not injure a human being, or through inaction, allow a human being to come to harm."

Fine, there need be no caviling about the kind of a human

being. It wouldn't matter whether they were male or female, short or tall, old or young, wise or foolish. Anything that can define a human being biologically will suffice.

The Second Law is a different matter altogether: "A robot must obey orders given it by a human being except where that would conflict with the First Law."

That has always made me uneasy. Suppose a robot on board ship is given an order by someone who knows nothing about ships, and that order would put the ship and everyone on board into danger. Is the robot obliged to obey? Of course not. Obedience would conflict with the First Law since human beings would be put into danger.

That assumes, however, that the robot knows everything about ships and can tell that the order is a dangerous one. Suppose, however, that the robot is not an expert on ships, but is experienced only in, let us say, automobile manufacture. He happens to be on board ship and is given an order by some landlubber and he doesn't know whether the order is safe or not.

It seems to me that he ought to respond, "Sir, since you have no knowledge as to the proper handling of ships, it would not be safe for me to obey any order you may give me involving such handling."

Because of that, I have often wondered if the Second Law ought to read, "A robot must obey orders given it by *qualified* human beings . . ."

But then I would have to imagine that robots are equipped with definitions of what would make humans "qualified" under different situations and with different orders. In fact, what if a landlubber robot on board ship is given orders by someone concerning whose qualifications the robot is totally ignorant.

Must he answer, "Sir, I do not know whether you are a qualified human being with respect to this order. If you can satisfy me that you are qualified to give me an order of this sort, I will obey it."

Then, too, what if the robot is faced by a child of ten—indisputably human as far as the First Law is concerned. Must the robot obey without question the orders of such a child, or the orders of a moron, or the orders of a man lost in the quagmire of emotion and beside himself?

The problem of when to obey and when not to obey is so complicated and devilishly uncertain that I have rarely subjected my robots to these equivocal situations.

And that brings me to the matter of aliens.

The physiological difference between aliens and ourselves matters to us—but then tiny physiological or even cultural differences between one human being and another also matter. To Smith and Campbell, ancestry obviously mattered; to others skin color matters, or gender or eye shape or religion or language or, for goodness sake, even hairstyle.

It seems to me that to decent human beings, none of these superficialities ought to matter. The Declaration of Independence states that "All men are created equal." Campbell, of course, argued with me many times that all men are manifestly *not* equal, and I steadily argued that they were all equal *before the law*. If a law was passed that stealing was illegal, then *no* man could steal. One couldn't say, "Well, if you went to Harvard and were a seventh-generation American you can steal up to one hundred thousand dollars; if you're an immigrant from the British Isles, you can steal up to one hundred dollars; but if you're of Polish birth, you can't steal at all." Even Campbell would admit that much (except that his technique was to change the subject).

And, of course, when we say that "All men are created equal" we are using "men" in the generic sense including both sexes and all ages, subjected to the qualification that a person must be mentally equipped to understand the difference between right and wrong.

In any case, it seems to me that if we broaden our perspective to consider non-human intelligent beings, then we must dismiss, as irrelevant, physiological and biochemical differences and ask only what the status of intelligence might be.

In short, a robot must apply the Laws of Robotics to any intelligent biological being, whether human or not.

Naturally, this is bound to create difficulties. It is one thing to design robots to deal with a specific non-human intelligence, and specialize in it, so to speak. It is quite another to have a robot encounter an intelligent species whom it has never met before.

After all, different species of living things may be intelligent to different extents, or in different directions, or subject to different modifications. We can easily imagine two intelligences with two utterly different systems of morals or two utterly different systems of senses.

Must a robot who is faced with a strange intelligence evaluate it only in terms of the intelligence for which he is programmed? (To put it in simpler terms, what if a robot, carefully trained to understand and speak French, encounters someone who can only understand and speak Farsi?)

Or suppose a robot must deal with individuals of two widely different species, each manifestly intelligent. Even if he understands both sets of languages, must he be forced to decide which of the two is the *more* intelligent before he can decide what to do in the face of conflicting orders—or which set of moral imperatives is the worthier?

Someday, this may be something I will have to take up in a story but, if so, it will give me a lot of trouble. Meanwhile, the whole point of the Robot City volumes is that young writers have the opportunity to take up the problems I have so far ducked. I'm delighted when they do. It gives them excellent practice and may teach me a few things, too.

A SYNOPSIS OF ROBOT CITY, BOOKS 1–6

He woke up . . . somewhere.

He didn't know where he was or how he had managed to get there. He didn't remember *anything* of his past.

Not even his name.

He was in some small capsule without windows. He could not even see where he was going.

His awakening had stirred a computer into life, and through its positronic personality he found that he was in a Massey lifepod. A badge on his clothing identified him as Derec—the name seemed to fit as well as anything. The positronic intelligence built into the lifepod could help him with very little; it had no information to aid him at all, not even the name of the ship from which it had been ejected.

The lifepod had landed on an asteroid that Derec quickly found was inhabited by a colony of robots. He seemed to be the only human there. The robots were as little help to him as the lifepod. Strangely silent about their task, they ignored him for the most part. They were obviously looking for something buried in the rock of the asteroid—it seemed to be the only explanation. While he tried to decipher just what it was they were looking for and why, a raider ship appeared.

While the robot colony prepared to self-destruct, Derec made a desperate attempt to escape from the asteroid and contact the raider.

As he was doing so, the raider's bombardment uncovered a shiny silver object, perhaps five centimeters by fifteen centimeters. He would later learn that it was called a "Key to Perihelion." A pursuing robot revealed that this was the object for which the robots were so obsessively searching.

Derec grabbed the Key and jumped. With the power of his augmented worksuit and the almost nonexistent gravity of the asteroid, he reached escape velocity, angling for the raider. But suddenly his faceplate was filled with a glaring blue light, and he was knocked unconscious.

He awoke on the raider ship and was confronted by a strange creature: wolf-like but with fingers instead of paws and a flattened, fur-covered face. The alien's name, as best he could pronounce it, was Wolruf. The creature escorted Derec to Aranimas, the captain of the raider ship, which seemed to be a jumble of half a dozen or more ships welded together in a patchwork maze.

Aranimas was also an alien, a humanoid of the Erani race, and very dangerous. Using a form of electrical prod, he tortured Derec to gain information as to what the robots were doing on the asteroid. Derec, of course, could tell him nothing. Aranimas then ordered Derec to put together a working robot from the salvaged parts from the asteroid and other raids.

Through Wolruf, Derec learned that Aranimas intended to replace the subservient Narwe race (who functioned as Aranimas's crew) with even more docile robots. Derec found that he did indeed seem to know a great deal about robotics; the knowledge came naturally to him. He managed to salvage one positronic brain and enough working parts to create a patchwork robot he called Alpha. The most curious thing about the robot was one of its arms: made of tiny cellular surfaces that seemed infinitely malleable, it could literally shape itself into any form needed. Derec remembered that many of the structures on the asteroid bore that same unique design, and he was filled with a desire to meet the inventor of this new substance.

Aranimas's constant mistreatment of Derec, Wolruf, and the Narwe made Derec determined to escape. With the use of Alpha, he and Wolruf successfully mutinied against Aranimas.

They also met another prisoner on the ship, a human female named Katherine Ariel Burgess. Derec recovered the Key to Perihelion, and they escaped Aranimas's ship, landing on a refueling station.

There Derec learned that Kate claimed to know something of his past but stubbornly refused to talk to him about it. He learned too, that she was suffering from some type of debilitating disease herself, and she also refused to talk about that.

The robots on the refueling station had taken the Key to Perihelion, and now it seemed that the bureaucrats who ran the Spacer society were also after the Key. Derec, with Ariel and Wolruf's help, recovered it. Through a mistake, Kate activated the Key while Derec was holding it. In an instant, the two were transported to Perihelion, a cold, formless place of gray fog. Pressing the switch on the Key again, they found themselves on top of a huge pyramidal tower in the middle of a city.

The Compass Tower of Robot City.

They were to find that Robot City was an intriguing place. The material of which it was composed was shaped like tiny Keys of Perihelion, and the city itself was undergoing constant change. Buildings would appear and move overnight. There was a constant blaze of activity by the millions of robots in the city, who claimed to be preparing this place for human inhabitants, though at the moment, the only humans here were Derec and Kate.

The city was in trouble. Nightly deluges raced through the streets, uncontrollable. Huge lightning storms daily menaced them. And there was a murdered human, a human named David who had looked exactly like Derec. Derec slowly realized that the city—as one robotic entity—was responding to what it considered to be a Third Law threat to its existence. The threat was David's blood; more specifically, the microbes in it. The rainstorms were a byproduct of the city's enormous and uncontrolled growth in response to that perceived threat. To save the city, he reprogrammed the central computer core to deactivate the city's defenses.

At the same time, Kate made an effort to recover the Key

to Perihelion, which she had hidden in the Compass Tower. It was gone. She and Derec were trapped here.

They found that the city robots had taken the original Key and were making duplicates of it. In the course of trying to steal one of the Keys, Derec and Kate began to develop a trust for each other.

Kate admitted to Derec that her real name was Ariel Welsh. She was the daughter of a wealthy Auroran patron of the sciences. Her mother had furnished one Dr. Avery the funds to design and build his pet project. Avery was an eccentric, argumentative genius who wanted to create on-going, self-sufficient cities to seed the stars for humankind. Avery, though, had disappeared. Robot City, Ariel guessed, was his original experiment, now running without Avery's control. As for Ariel, she had been banished from Aurora because of her incurable disease, contracted from a Spacer. Given a ship and funds by her mother, she'd gone looking for a cure.

It was imperative for her to leave Robot City if she was going to live.

In the meantime, Robot City had acquired another human visitor: Jeff Leong, whose ship had exploded just outside the atmosphere. He was badly injured; to save him, the robots of Robot City turned him into a cyborg: a human brain encased in a robotic body. Insufficient knowledge of the bio-chemical structure of the brain led to Jeff's slow insanity, though otherwise the surgery was a complete success.

Alpha and Wolruf had also made their way to the city via a modified Massey lifepod, big enough for only one human.

With Alpha and Wolruf's help, Derec and Ariel were able to capture the increasingly violent and unstable cyborg. Using Derec's body as a model, the medical technicians of Robot City were able to transplant Jeff's brain back into his own newly healed body. However, he remained ill and largely out of his senses.

Alpha, during the capture of Jeff, had received instructions from the cellular material in his flexible arm ordering the robot to change its name to Mandelbrot. Derec suspected that the arm, from an Avery-style robot, might well have also sent a signal to Avery to return to Robot City.

A choice had to be made: let Ariel take the lifepod and escape, or send Jeff back. Ariel insisted that Jeff must be the one to go.

Robot City continued its fascinating evolution. Not long after Jeff's departure, the behavior of the robots began to show definitely odd tendencies. Circuit Breaker appeared: a building like two four-sided pyramids stuck together at their bases and balanced on one point. The building, the first work of creative art built by a robot, reflected ever-changing colors as it rotated. Three robots, calling themselves the Three Cracked Cheeks, formed a Dixieland jazz band. All this came about as an effort by the city to formulate what it called the Laws of Humanics—corollaries to the Three Laws of Robotics. The Laws of Humanics were supposed to govern—or at least explain—the actions of human beings as the Three Laws of Robotics governed those of positronic intelligence.

The most serious and unusual event in all the strangeness was that a robot was murdered by another robot. Lucius, the creator of Circuit Breaker, was found with all its positronic circuitry deliberately destroyed, so that the brain could never be reconstructed. It seemed a deliberate attempt to stifle the advances made by the Avery robots.

In the midst of this, Avery himself returned to the city, and Derec, Ariel, Wolruf, and Mandelbrot quickly discovered that the doctor was a dangerous megalomaniac. All that mattered to Avery was his work; he could not have cared less about Ariel's illness or the plight of the others. All that mattered to him was Robot City. He had stationed Hunter-Seeker robots around the area to take all of them prisoner until he could analyze all that had happened here—in whatever way was most convenient to him.

They were taken prisoner, and Derec, unknowingly, was given a dose of chemfets: miniature replicas of the city material that took residence in his bloodstream.

Escaping at last, Derec, Ariel, Wolruf, and Mandelbrot left Robot City on Dr. Avery's ship. There, in a hidden compartment, they found a Key to Perihelion.

• • •

It was obvious that Avery anticipated their escape, for the ship was sabotaged. Without the ability to home in on the navigational beacons, they could not program the jumps through hyperspace. Ariel had also taken a definite turn for the worse. Derec decided that he and Ariel must use the Key to Perihelion to try to get help for her. Wolruf and Mandelbrot would remain with the ship and try to complete repairs or attract help from another ship.

Derec activated the Key, and he and Ariel found themselves in an apartment on Earth. They found Earth society paranoid and isolated, with extremely xenophobic attitudes toward Spacers. However, Ariel was getting progressively weaker, and Derec in desperation took her to a local hospital. If Earth was backward in some ways, it seemed that its medical facilities were better than Aurora's. They recognized her disease—amnemonic plague—and cured her.

Unfortunately, the chemfets in Derec's body were asserting their presence, and he was rapidly getting weaker himself. With the help of R. David, an Earth robot, they stole a ship from an Earth spaceport and headed out to rescue Wolruf and Mandelbrot.

Another spaceship followed them: Aranimas, who had tracked the bursts of Key static to Earth. In a tense battle, Derec and Ariel, with Mandelbrot and Wolruf, managed to destroy Aranimas's ship at great cost to their own vessels. They had only one option left to them with Derec growing weaker: use the Key to jump back to Robot City.

They emerged from the Compass Tower into Avery's vacant office, intending to force the doctor into helping Derec. To find him, Wolruf and Mandelbrot went into the city, while Derec and Ariel began searching the tunnels underneath the tower.

Mandelbrot and Wolruf found that the robots were all following the orders of what they called the Migration Program. They were leaving the first Robot City and seeking new worlds on which to build. And when they returned to Compass Tower, they found that Hunter-Seeker robots were searching for Derec and Ariel, who had fled.

Above the planet, a small spacecraft arrived, carrying Jeff

Leong. Back to normal, he was returning to rescue the others. Meeting with Derec and company, he was determined to help them find Dr. Avery.

It was actually Dr. Avery who found them, the Hunter-Seeker robots capturing the company one by one. The Doctor revealed that Derec was actually David Avery, Dr. Avery's son, and that the chemfets in his body would one day allow him to control every Avery robot in existence. Derec would *become* Robot City.

But Avery had believed Derec would be a willing partner in his plans. He was very wrong in that. Derec used his new control of the city to free his companions; Dr. Avery triggered a Key to Perihelion before he could be captured. He fled into the void.

Derec and the others gave no thought to pursuit. At last, they were safe and free to leave.

It seemed reward enough. . . .

ISAAC ASIMOV'S ROBOT CITY™

ROBOTS AND ALIENS

Changeling

CHAPTER 1
BIRTH

"I feel uneasy about this, Dr. Anastasi."

Janet Anastasi glanced up with a half-smile. She brushed blond hair back from bright, hazel eyes cupped in smile lines. "And just how does a robot feel 'uneasy,' Basalom?" she asked with a laugh.

Basalom's eyes blinked, a shutter membrane flickering momentarily over the optical circuits. Janet had deliberately built in that random quirk. She built idiosyncracies into all her robots—eccentricities of speech, of mannerisms. The foibles seemed to make Basalom and the rest less mechanically predictable. To her, they lent the robots individual personalities they otherwise lacked.

"The term is simply an approximation, Doctor."

"Hmm." She wiped sweat from her forehead with the back of her hand and wiped it on the leg of her pants. "Give me a hand with this, will you, my friend?"

The two were in the cargo hold of a small ship. A viewscreen on one wall showed the mottled blue-and-white curve of the planet they were orbiting. Twin moons peered over the shoulder of the world, and the land mass directly below them was green with foliage. It seemed a pastoral land from this distance, no matter what the reality might actually be. Janet knew that the atmosphere of the world was within terran norms, that the earth was fertile, and that there was life, though without any signs of technology: the ship's instruments had told her that much. The world, whatever the inhabitants might call it, fit her needs. Beyond that, she didn't care.

Her husband of many years ago, Wendell Avery, had said during their breakup that she didn't care about anything made of simple flesh—not him, not their son. "You're afraid to love something that might love you back," he'd raged.

"Which makes us exactly the same, doesn't it?" she'd shouted back at him. "Or can't the genius admit that he has faults? Maybe it's just because you don't like the fact that *I'm* the one who's considered the robotic expert? That's it, isn't it, Wendell? *You* can't love anyone else because your own self-worship takes up all the space in your heart."

His remark had made her furious at the time, but time had softened the edges of her anger. Avery might be a conceited, egocentric ass, but there had been some truth in what he'd said. She'd looked in that mirror too often and seen herself backing away from contact with other people to be with her robots. Surely she'd been content here on this ship for the last few years, with only Basalom and a few other robots for company.

Avery she missed not at all; her son sometimes she missed terribly. Basalom and the others had become her surrogate children.

"Gently," she cautioned Basalom. A spheroid of silvery-gray metal approximately two meters in diameter sat on the workbench before her, its gleaming surface composed of tiny dodecahedral segments. She'd just finished placing the delicate, platinum-iridium sponge of a positronic brain into a casing within the lumpy sphere. Now Basalom draped the sticky lace of the neural connections over the brain and sealed the top half of the casing. The geometric segments molded together seamlessly.

"You can put it in the probe," Janet told the robot, then added: "What's this about being uneasy?"

"You have built me very well, Doctor; that is the only reason I sense anything at all. I am aware of a millisecond pause in my positronic relays due to possible First Law conflicts," Basalom replied as he carefully lifted the sphere and moved it to the launching tube. "While there is no imminent danger of lock-up, nor is this sufficient to cause any danger of malfunction or loss of effectiveness, it's my understanding that humans feel a similar effect when presented with an action that presents a moral conflict. Thus, my use of the human term."

Janet grinned, deepening the lines netting her eyes. "Long-winded, but logical enough, I suppose."

Basalom blinked again. "Brevity is more desired than accuracy when speaking of human emotions?"

That elicited a quick laugh. "Sometimes, Basalom. Sometimes. It's a judgment call, I'm afraid. Sometimes it doesn't matter what you say so long as you just talk."

"I am not a good judge when it comes to human emotions, Doctor."

"Which puts you in company with most of us, I'm afraid." Janet clamped the seals on the probe's surface and patted it affectionately. LEDs glowed emerald on the launching tube's panel as she closed the access.

"What does a human being do when he or she is uneasy, Doctor Anastasi?"

Janet shrugged, stepping back. "It depends. If you believe in something, you go ahead with it. You trust your judgment and ignore the feeling. If you never have any doubts, you're either mad or not thinking things through."

"Then you have reservations about your experiment as well, but you will still launch the probe."

"Yes," she answered. "If people were so paralyzed by doubt that they never did anything without being certain of the outcome, there'd never be children, after all."

As Janet watched, Basalom seemed to ponder that. The robot moved a step closer to the controls for the launching tube; its hand twitched—another idiosyncracy. The robot seemed to be on the verge of wanting to say more. The glimmer of a thought struck her. "Basalom?"

"Yes, Doctor?"

"Would *you* care to launch this probe?"

Blink. Twitch. For a moment, the robot didn't move. Janet thought perhaps it would not, then the hand reached out and touched the contact. "Thank you, Doctor," Basalom said, and pressed.

Serried lights flashed; there was a *chuff* of escaping air, and the probe was flung into the airless void beyond. Basalom turned to watch it on the viewscreen; Janet watched him.

"You never said what your reservations were exactly, Basalom," she noted.

"These new robots—with your programming, so much is left for them to decide. Yes, the Three Laws are imbedded in the positronic matrix, but you have given them no definition of 'human.'"

"You wonder what will happen?"

"If they one day encounter human beings, will they recognize them? Will they respond as they are supposed to respond?"

Janet shrugged. "I don't know. That's the beauty of it, Basalom. I don't know."

"If you say so, Doctor. But I don't understand that concept."

"They're seeds. Formless, waiting seeds coded only with the laws. They don't even know they're robots. I'm curious to see what they grow up to be, my friend."

Janet turned and watched the hurtling probe wink in sunlight as it tumbled away from the ship. It dwindled as it fell into the embrace of the world's gravity and was finally lost in atmospheric glare. Janet sighed.

"This one's planted," she said. She took a deep breath. "Now let's get out of here," she said.

CHAPTER 2
THE DOPPLEGANGER

The probe lay encased in mud halfway down a hillside. The once-silvery sides were battered and scorched from the long fall through the atmosphere; drying streamers of black earth coated the dented sides. Ghostly heat waves shimmered, and the metallic hull ticked as it cooled and contracted. The echoes of its landing reverberated for a long time among the hills.

Inside the abused shell, timed relays opened and fed power to the positronic circuitry of the robot nestled in its protective cradle. The neophyte mind found itself in total darkness. Had it been a living creature, its birth instincts would have taken over like a sea turtle burrowing from the wet sand to find the shimmering sea. The robot had its own instinct-analogue— the Three Laws of Robotics. Knowledge of these basic rules flooded the robot's brightening awareness.

First Law: A robot may not harm a human being, or, through inaction, allow a human being to come to harm.

Second Law: A robot must obey the orders given it by human beings except where such orders would conflict with the First Law.

Third Law: A robot must protect its own existence as long

as such protection does not interfere with the First or Second Laws.

This was the manner in which most of known human space defined the Laws. Any schoolchild of Aurora or Earth or Solaris could have recited them by rote. But to the fledgling, there was one important, essential difference. To the fledgling, there were no *words* involved, only deep, core compulsions. The fledgling had no sense that it had been built or that it was merely a constructed machine.

It didn't think of itself as a robot.

It only knew that it had certain instructions it must obey.

As survival instincts, the Laws were enough to spark a response. Second Law governed the fledgling's first reactions, enhanced by Third Law resonance. There were imperious voices in its mind: inbuilt programming, speaking a language it knew instinctively. The robot followed the instructions given it, and more circuits opened.

An opening appeared in the probe's hull, and the fledgling allowed itself to roll out. The skin of its body shimmered, the myriad dodecahedral segments flexing and shifting as it stretched like warm putty. The robot extruded pseudopods to stabilize the round body. Sensory input was taken in through the skin: optical, auditory, tactile, scent. At the same time, a larger store of basic files was released into the receptive mind: a heavily edited encyclopedia of carefully chosen knowledge. It paused, searching the programming as it absorbed impressions of its surroundings.

A voice whispered.

Move away from the landing site. Beings may come to investigate; they may be aggressive and dangerous. Hide.

Which left the problem: how to move? The positronic brain searched the files and found an answer. The skin molded itself further, the pseudopods becoming muscular legs. The robot scuttled away quickly, moving uphill to a stand of coarse, tall grass. Its round body flattened, the legs retracted; it hunkered down, patient.

As it waited, it inventoried itself dispassionately. The Three Laws overlaid everything else in its mind, but there was more. Most of its programming, and indeed this very self-evaluation, seemed to be manifestations of the Third Law. It must protect its own existence; to survive, it must learn as much as possible.

Underneath the Laws was the layer of initial programming, most of which the fledgling had already followed in the first few minutes of life. Beneath that was a substrate of complex if/then branches. The robot ignored most of those—they all fed back into the Laws in any case.

Only one set of impulses was immediately needed, and that flowed directly from the Laws. *A robot may not harm a human being. A robot must obey the orders given it by human beings*, the Laws insisted. But what was a human being?

The programming gave an answer, not a definition but a description: *A human being is an intelligent lifeform.* So the fledgling, not knowing what a "robot" was other than a term that applied to itself, knew it had to find human beings, to protect and serve them. It had to search out an intelligent lifeform.

It began to formulate a strategy.

The fledgling didn't move; it continued to wait. Intelligence of necessity implied curiosity. An intelligent lifeform in the immediate area would have seen the fiery, noisy descent. It would come to investigate the fall. If no life that met the criterion arrived, then the fledgling would look elsewhere.

The area in which the probe had landed was heavily forested. Tightly packed trees with large, blue-green fronds huddled nearby and surrounded the grassy, hillside meadow. The area was alive with sound now, and the robot could see movement in the twilight under the swaying canopy of leaves. The air was temperate and fragrant with damp earth; the sound of running water trilled not far away. This was a good place, the robot decided. Human beings—whatever they might be— would probably find this location pleasant. Had they come here, they might well have stayed.

Afternoon faded to evening. The robot saw several creatures on the hillside, but none displayed any undue interest in the pod. Once, something with a thin, furred body approached. On muscular hind legs, it stretched out a long, four-fingered hand to touch the pod, and the robot saw a marsupial pouch on its stomach. Though the versatile hand made the robot watch closely, the creature did nothing to reveal more than animal intelligence. It wore no clothing, had no tools, and the robot's sensitive hearing recorded only meaningless grunts from the beast. The marsupial glanced around with wide, scarlet-pupiled eyes, nostril slits flapping on its wide, flat head. Then it went back down on all fours and bounded off. The fledgling decided not to follow. Not yet.

Nightfall came with a surprising quickness after the sun slipped behind the trees; the air temperature dropped as rapidly. The forest settled into relative quiet as the nocturnal creatures woke and began to prowl. The night was well lit. The larger of the two moons was full; the smaller, at three-quarters, rose not long after full night.

Somewhere under the trees, a series of coughing barks rose, long and highly modulated. The robot began to listen closely as the call came again, slightly changed. Another voice answered the first, shorter and deeper; then yet another, followed by a shivering howl. The intonations were complex and varied, yet obviously from the same species. Already the fledgling had identified repetitive "syllables" in the phrases.

Twin-shadowed creatures moved under the margins of the trees, sleek and fast. The fledgling counted five of them, though more may have been lurking farther back in the forest. One of the pack broke away from the group, moving into moonlight.

The creature was caninoid. At least, it came closest to matching that type in the inbuilt files of the robot's brain. That meant little in itself. There was nothing in the robot's programmed knowledge that said a "human being" could not be canine. Standing on four legs, the animal stood a meter from shoulder to ground, powerfully built and broad-chested. The fur was mottled gray and black, glossy with silvered tips; the head was short-muzzled and round, with a large skull and wide-set, light eyes. The tail was long and furless; it looked nearly prehensile. As the robot watched, the creature howled again as if in challenge, revealing molars set well back behind a double rank of incisors—an omnivore, possibly, not strictly a meat-eater. The front legs ended in a clawed paw, but the toes/fingers were long, separate, and articulated, with a definite closing thumb for grasping. The thick elbow joints seemed capable of a wide range of motion.

It stared at the pod gleaming in doubled moonlight. It reared up on its hind legs (a female, the robot noted). With a stabbing motion of her front paw, she gestured: a wave.

Moonlight glinted on something on the creature's chest, and the fledgling adjusted its vision to see the thing more clearly: a long, curved fang, hanging on a string of braided vine. *Artifact!* The word screamed in the fledgling's mind, but she continued to wait.

Four others came out of the cover of the trees now, one gray-furred ancient, two adults, and a youngling. They moved swiftly to the sides of the first but carefully stayed behind her. The adults paced, restless. The ancient jabbered: half bark, half growl. The leader shook her head. The old one barked again, and the leader turned with a growl, showing her teeth. She cuffed at the old one, but the raking claws missed as the elder cowered back and lifted her muzzle to bare the throat in submission. The leader turned her back on the others and stared again at the pod. She approached the crumpled metal, snuffling.

She sat before it.

The tail served as support, and its agile tip curled around the back feet. The creature cocked her head to one side then the other. She sniffed again, leaning closer to the pod, then reached out with her left paw. Talons clicked on metal; she tapped the surface, listening to the faint, hollow ringing.

What she did next made synapses open in the robot's positronic mind.

The tail flicked and curled around a small stick on the ground near the pod. The stick was brought up; she took it in her paw, clasping it between the thumb and two fingers. Leaning forward, she placed the tip of the stick under a torn flap of metal and levered up a strand of foil insulation. She pulled it loose and sat back to examine it, letting the stick drop.

Tool use. Coupled with the intricate language, the necklace the leader wore and their curiosity about the probe, that was enough evidence. They were intelligent; that also meant that they were human beings.

With that decision, the unformed body of the fledgling began to take on definite shape, as if unseen hands were molding clay while using the creatures before it as models. First, the basic wolf-like shape, the muscular leanness. The head extruded, rounded, then pushed out the snout of a nose and the flaps of ears. Fixed optical lenses focused in deep-set eye-sockets, colored the same startling ice blue. It could not fully imitate fur, but the surface texture roughened, and the reflective patterns altered so that it displayed a vaguely similar silver-gray and black pattern. After a moment of pondering, the robot also mimicked the secondary sexual characteristics of the leader. The behavior of the leader suggested that scent was an important sense to them. That was simple enough. A quick sampling of the leader's pheromones, and tiny artificial glands secreted an artificial wolf scent.

A gentle breeze was blowing downslope. The leader raised her head suddenly. She went down on all fours, and her lips drew back to bare the dangerous fangs. She growled, staring up the hill to the stand of grass where the robot waited.

The robot stepped out to meet them.

At the same time, without warning, the leader howled and charged.

CHAPTER 3

The wolf-creature's attack was maddeningly swift, but the fledgling's reflexes were still faster. She had no time to retreat, only to react. The Third Law compelled the robot to move so as to protect herself while the First Law stopped her from harming the wolf-creature in return. As the snarling leader leapt toward the robot, the fledgling rolled so that her powerful jaws snapped shut on air, and the claws barely touched the metallic body. Even so, the force of the blow sent the robot flailing in the dirt before she found her balance again.

The fledgling bounded to her feet, turning, but the leader —strangely—hadn't followed up her advantage. Crouching, the wolf-creature bared her teeth once more at the robot and uttered a quick growl that was obviously a command. The Second Law demanded that a human being be obeyed, and the fledgling had made the decision that the creatures were human. Yet without understanding the language, she could only guess as to what was being said.

She remembered how the leader had challenged the old one in the pack. She patterned her behavior after the ancient's: she bared her throat submissively and backed away.

11

The ploy worked. The leader sniffed again, growled softly deep in her throat, and turned. She padded down the hill without looking back. Halfway to her followers, she stopped and glared back up the slope to the fledgling, standing motionless under the twin moons. The robot took a step in the leader's direction; the "human" turned once again and continued on down the hill.

The invitation was clear. It seemed more dangerous to ignore her than to follow, so the robot did so, imitating the leader's silent, fluid gait. Once the leader approached the other wolf-creatures again, the pack reformed. The body language and demeanor of the others told the robot that an established pecking order denoted precedence within the pack. There was a well-defined hierarchy in which a newcomer, by all indications, took the lowest rung. Even the juveniles bared teeth as the fledgling approached, and she hung well back as the leader barked commands. The wolf-creatures turned as one and slid quickly back under the cover of moonlit trees.

The fledgling followed closely behind.

Under the trees, the pack moved quietly and furtively. They had obviously been interrupted in the middle of a hunt. Just inside the trees, three young wolf-creatures waited for them. A flint knife hung from each of their necks, and they were yoked to primitive *travois*, long poles of dead branches lashed together with vines. The *travois* held the fragrant, butchered carcasses of dead animals. Each bump caused a cloud of black insects to rise from the meat.

The fledgling stayed with the pack easily; somehow, it felt *right* to be moving this way under the double shadows beneath the slow rustling of the leaves—having decided the wolf-creatures were human, her mind was already adopting their patterns as correct. The youngest of the juvenile carriers slackened his pace not long after they left the clearing of the pod, dropping back until he was abreast the fledgling with his burden. He made an inquisitive soft bark as they ran behind the others; when the fledgling didn't answer, he repeated the sound.

He was obviously waiting for a response, yet the fledgling had no idea what was appropriate. She knew only one language—that of the words inside her head. She could give names to the things she saw around her, could even speak them aloud if she wished. She gave no thought to where that language came from; it simply was.

The problem was translation, to change her language into words these creatures used. She knew that once she got them to talk, she would quickly acquire a vocabulary. The robotic memory would forget nothing it heard; the positronic intelligence would discover syntax and grammar rapidly.

But without input, there was only a void. A void was dangerous to her, and that was anathema to the Third Law. If she understood them and if she could communicate easily, there would be a lessening of danger. She had to make them speak enough for her to start acquiring the knowledge she needed.

The adolescent was waiting for her response, staring at her as he pulled the *travois* through the quiet woods. The fledgling did what her programming decided was the highest percentage action. She imitated the sound the young male had made.

The effect was not what she desired. The youngster glared at her with a rolling of pastel blue eyes, sniffed disgustedly, and increased his speed to put distance between himself and the robot. She let him go.

For a long time, they wound their way through the paths of the forest.

The largest moon had set before the leader came to a halt deep in the forest and several kilometers from the landing site. The forest had gone dark and tangled. Large vines spun leafy webbings from the trees; the underbrush was thick and prickled with thorns. A cold dew frothed the edges of leaves, sparkling in the blue-white gleam of the remaining moon and spilling down on the pack from above. The fur of the wolf-creatures was beaded with it.

The leader prowled the edges of the clearing as the others sat on their haunches, tongues lolling and their breath steaming in the night air. The fledgling imitated them, watching as the leader sniffed the air in evident agitation. The robot sampled the air; there was a faint trace of a bitter animal scent below that of the wolf-creatures and their kill.

Nearby, a mass of tiny white-winged moths spiraled and danced in a shaft of moonlight. A sloth-like animal capered along the pathway of tree limbs, shaking down more of the dew. The forest was almost too quiet. The panting of the pack seemed very loud.

Beyond the clearing came a thrashing of leaves and the sharp crack of a branch breaking underfoot. The bitter smell was suddenly very intense.

The moths abandoned their mad cavort and fled silently.

The leader barely had time to growl a warning.

A nightmare vision burst through the trees nearest the leader. There was a glimpse of red, nearly phosphorescent eyes set in a head that looked as if it had been crushed: wide and flat with an impossibly long jaw bristling with rows of knife-edged fangs, fangs that the fledgling recognized as the same as the one that hung on the leader's necklace. Below, two sets of reptilian, long-fingered claws flailed. The thing moved on thick back legs, larger by far than any of the pack, its stout body armored with beaded hard scales. A muscular tail whipped around it, tearing into the undergrowth.

It saw the pack, shrieked thinly, and charged. A fierce blow of the claws raked the leader's shoulder, and she yelped in dismay. She crouched, ready to attack, but was obviously overmatched.

A blur of motion passed her.

The fledgling had begun to move from the first sight of the apparition, powered by the First Law.

Another robot, patterned after the moral codes of *homo sapiens*, might only have restrained the creature. But the fledgling was already adopting the mental patterns she had seen in her "humans." She was a carnivore, a hunter.

She slammed into the side of the thing as it readied to snap at the leader. Powerful as the beast was, its strength was overmatched by the robot's, and her new form seemed admirably suited to complement her mechanical power. Her teeth clamped down on the beast's arm and twisted savagely. The thing bellowed in pain and reared back.

Still, the creature was too large, too bulky. A flick of its arm threw her off as it roared in fury. The huge mouth opened, giving off a stench of ancient, rotting meat. The beast snapped at the fledgling, but she had already moved. As it turned to find her, she leapt again, this time at the long neck of the beast. She hesitated as her jaws closed around it. But already the others in the pack were attacking. If she hesitated, if she waited any longer, they might be injured.

She put pressure on her jaws and felt the windpipe collapse beneath her crushing jaws.

The beast fell, choking. The rest of the pack swarmed over the body, tearing at it.

All but the leader. Panting, she regarded the fledgling, and there seemed to be little sympathy in her stance. The forepaws were braced, as if she were waiting for an attack. The dark lips were drawn back slightly from the gums to reveal the ivory teeth, and a low, relentless growling came from her throat. The fang at her neck swung softly from side to side.

The fledgling didn't move. It seemed best to stand absolutely still. The leader's icy stare remained on her for long seconds, while the rest of the pack ripped apart the body of the reptilian beast, while they reformed into a ragged line, while the younglings were strapped back into the *travois*.

At last, the old one barked a query. The leader seemed to ponder what had been said. Then her gaze moved away from the fledgling, almost disdainfully. She padded back to the head of the pack and howled. They readied themselves to move on again.

This time, the youngling meat carriers waited for the fledgling to go first. The pack left her a space well up toward the leader. The old wolf-creature moved alongside her. Just before they left the clearing, the old one pointed at the tattered body of the reptile. "*Hrrringa*," he said throatily, then repeated the word.

"*Hrrringa*." The fledgling spoke the strange word, also pointing. Hrrringa: reptile creature.

The old one nodded. His eyes, rheumy and bloodshot, narrowed with pleasure as the pack began to move again.

By the time the pack stopped to sleep in the early morning, the fledgling had learned several more words.

PackHome.

That was what the old one (the fledgling had learned that his name was LifeCrier) called the cave dimpling a rocky hillside deep in the forest. PackHome was where all litter-kin—those of the same pack—dwelled. The fledgling had picked up a name among the kin herself: she would be known as SilverSide, LifeCrier decided, for her flanks gleamed like the scales of a fish, and like a fish her skin was hard and cold. The name seemed right.

"You killed the *hrrringa*, the SharpFang, and saved Keen-Eye's life," LifeCrier reminded the robot in KinSpeech. Following KeenEye's lead, the group from the Hunt loped from the cover of trees and started up the long slope to the cave of PackHome. The moons (LargeFace and SmallFace, as the Hunt called them) had spent most of the night chasing one another behind wind-blown clouds. SmallFace peeked out from an opening and spilled light down on the pack.

"The news will spread quickly," LifeCrier continued. "You have status now. Don't bare your throat to any of the kin who weren't on the Hunt. You had the right to challenge KeenEye for leadership of the Hunt; even though you didn't do so, those at PackHome are all lower than you. Let them know your scent, but if one of them acts the superior, challenge them."

"I won't hurt litter-kin," SilverSide said. Already it felt natural to be speaking in their language. She was no longer simply translating from that odd internal vocabulary she'd somehow known from the beginning. "I can't."

LifeCrier let his tongue loll out between time-dulled teeth: amusement. "Don't worry about that. They'll back down and KeenEye has to support you. She owes you a life debt."

SilverSide had spent the last four days with the pack, moving through the forest and resting during the hot, bright days. She had helped them kill, watched them butcher the animals and send the younglings back home when the *travois* were full. She'd listened to them, always learning, as they complained about the lack of prey, as they licked wounds, as they groomed each other, as they talked about old fights and old hunts.

In the four nights SilverSide had spent with the wolf-creatures, she'd learned much of the complex language of the pack. It was a blend of body language, of modulated yelps and whines and barks. There were different modes of speech as well: the formal HuntTongue used between different packs or to stress superiority among litter-kin; an informal Kin-Speech used in PackHome or between friends; the simple BeastTalk, which had no words at all but only the high emotional content of the raw animal.

Underlying it all were the strong instincts of the pack carnivore, and the robot was rapidly absorbing that mindset. Already her interpretation of the Three Laws was unlike that of any humanoid positronic intelligence. A robotics engineer would have considered SilverSide dangerously unbalanced; one who knew what she'd done to the SharpFang in the forest and watched her behavior over the last several days would have been certain of it.

SilverSide could already see wolf-creatures crowding the opening to the cave, which glowed green in the darkness from phosphorescent moss the kin gathered and used for light. They yelped greetings to the Hunt in glad BeastTalk, and there were happy cries at the sight of game dragging behind the remaining carriers. KeenEye led the Hunt to the cave opening, then sat on her haunches as the rest of the pack spilled out. She began speaking quietly to two of the other kin.

There were ten or more litter-kin who came from the cave mouth, and SilverSide could hear and smell pups still inside. The ones who stayed in PackHome during the Hunt were the nursing mothers, the infirm, and the very young. Some of them were already taking meat from the carriers and moving it inside. Others greeted mates while the two youngest from the Hunt basked in the obvious adulation of the immature pups.

SilverSide noticed the sidewise glances from KeenEye and the others, the half-disguised scenting in her direction. She sat alongside LifeCrier, just behind KeenEye and out of the press of kin. KeenEye glanced back at her with a hard stare.

"I've told the kin about you," she said in HuntTongue, and there was no kindness in her tone at all. "I've told them that you are to be treated as litter-kin. A place will be made for you in PackHome."

"Thank you," SilverSide replied—a quick bark and a nod of the head. SilverSide made her response as cold and formal as KeenEye's. The Hunt leader sniffed at that, nodded, and padded softly into PackHome.

SilverSide could smell LifeCrier's strange delight at the exchange. "She insults you by using the HuntTongue. You know that?"

"She is the leader," SilverSide answered. "That means I must obey her."

"She's still waiting for you to challenge her. I could almost taste the fear."

"Why would I challenge her?"

"You came from the Void," LifeCrier said. There was an eager lilt in his ancient voice, and he howled softly in Beast-Talk for a moment. "I saw the trail of fire as you fell from the SpiritWorld in the stone egg. You're the OldMother's offspring. You were sent to us, and so KeenEye waits for the spirit of OldMother to move you."

"I do not feel a spirit inside," SilverSide told the old kin.

"You came from the SpiritWorld," LifeCrier said again, as if that fact answered all objections.

"I do not know that, LifeCrier. There is no memory of it in me. I knew nothing before I crawled from the egg. I acted as it felt right to act. I saw KeenEye and the Hunt; it seemed important that I take on your shape."

"That was the spirit of OldMother speaking to you." Life-Crier tilted his graying head and gave a short, excited yip. "You've come as OldMother promised. You're the sign of forgiveness. You're her answer to the WalkingStones, and that's why KeenEye is afraid."

"The WalkingStones? I do not know the word. What are WalkingStones?"

LifeCrier had no chance to answer the robot's query. Keen-Eye came back out into the night air and trotted directly toward them. Rather than halting as she approached, she continued so that SilverSide and LifeCrier had to give way or be struck. KeenEye sat exactly where SilverSide had been sitting.

"The Hunt must go back out," she said in KinSpeech. "The meat we killed fills barely half the food cave. We wasted time finding the stone egg and SilverSide."

SilverSide said nothing, but LifeCrier gave a short bark of derision. "A waste of time that saved your life," he told KeenEye. "You should thank the OldMother for sending you such a waste."

KeenEye gave a low BeastTongue growl as SmallFace slid back into cloud cover. Her eyes were bright in the gloom, touched with flecks of green from the phosphorus around the cave mouth. The wind ruffled the long fur around her neck and brought the scent of forest. "Had we not gone looking for the egg, perhaps we would never have met the SharpFang and I would not have a life debt to SilverSide. And only an old litter-kin too ancient to sire pups says that OldMother sent the egg. But that doesn't matter. The Hunt has to feed the kin."

"You know that finding SilverSide wasn't the reason the meat was scarce. It's the Hill of Stars and the WalkingStones —that's what has made the prey scarce, and that's why Old-Mother sent SilverSide to us." LifeCrier was slipping into

HuntTongue, his words and posture becoming more stylized. "I, LifeCrier, say this because the AllSpirit lives in me. I will not let KeenEye deceive the litter-kin."

KeenEye snarled, showing her teeth. "Do *you* want to challenge me, old one? Do you want to lead the Hunt yourself? Fine, I'm ready."

Others of the litter-kin were filling the cleared area around the cave mouth, watching silently. SilverSide could scent the tension. Her senses were almost hyper-aware, driven by First Law programming that translated as a feeling of uneasiness. She readied herself to move, to come between LifeCrier and KeenEye if they began to fight.

But LifeCrier shook his grizzled head. "The AllSpirit told me that I was to speak the history of all kin, not lead the pack, KeenEye. That's why I am LifeCrier. I've no interest in challenging you. If you wish, I'll submit now." With that, Life-Crier lifted his head so that the throat was exposed to KeenEye. For a moment, the tableau held, KeenEye quivering on the edge of attack and SilverSide ready to intercept the leader's rush.

But KeenEye did nothing. Slowly, LifeCrier let his muzzle drop. His demeanor was haughty, knowing that he'd won this confrontation. "SilverSide is the gift of the OldMother," he declared loudly so that all the others could hear.

"The truth of that remains to be seen," KeenEye grumbled.

"Haven't the WalkingStones taken the lives of kin? Haven't they driven the prey from the forest around them? Haven't we seen pups starve and mothers' milk become thin? Haven't One-Eye's and ScarredPaw's packs warned us not to enter their territory, knowing how desperate we are?"

"Yes," KeenEye admitted, "but that says nothing about SilverSide."

"I know the old tales—I had them from the old LifeCrier, as he had them from the one before him on down through time. The spirits of kin past live in me. I know what I know." Again, LifeCrier began using the HuntTongue as if reciting a litany. "I saw the fiery egg leave a trail across the Void to lead the Hunt. When SilverSide revealed herself, we could all smell the scent of litter-kin. The AllSpirit woke in me as I tasted it."

LifeCrier rose up on his hind legs, pointing with a forepaw over the treetops to the west. "Look, we've seen the Hill of Stars from PackHome for ten Dances. Doesn't the sight of it make the fur rise on your back?"

Silverside looked to where the old one had pointed. Faintly, through the swaying foliage, she could see a triangular shape a long distance away. Its dim bulk was pricked with lights as bright as the stars. She adjusted her vision, bringing the thing into sharper focus. Unwinking rectangles of yellow light were set in a dark pyramid of stone. *Artifact*. There was no translation for that word in the language of kin. *Artifact*.

The vision filled her with a need to know more.

"The old tales have muddled your head," KeenEye was telling LifeCrier.

"The old tales begin to seem too much like now, I'd say instead," LifeCrier answered, and there was a soft rumble of agreement from the kin around them. "It is as if GrayMane walked again."

SilverSide tore her attention away from the sight of the Hill of Stars. "Who is GrayMane?" she asked. At that, KeenEye sniffed laughter.

"So OldMother's supposed offspring doesn't know the old tales," she spat. "I know them all too well. And I've little enough time to spend in PackHome to listen to them again." With a shake of her head, she rose and went into the cave. Most of the kin followed her, but a few remained behind on the ledge.

"Who is GrayMane?" SilverSide asked again.

LifeCrier had watched KeenEye's departure. Now he turned back to SilverSide and nodded. "I will tell you," he said formally. Raising his muzzle, he gave a long, mournful howl.

Listen, oh Kin! (LifeCrier began). Gather here and listen.

I speak of a time before time.

I speak to the spirits that live in you so they too will listen and know that we haven't forgotten them.

I speak of the ending days before the One Great Pack splintered.

In that long, last winter, two kin of the Final Litter, sister and brother, came to be possessed by their ancestor spirits. GrayMane was taken by the spirit of the OldMother (may Her name be praised), and, with the wisdom of the OldMother, she became the first of us to speak the language of the Kin. SplitEar, her brother, was taken by the spirit of the First-Beast, and thus he spoke no language at all.

This is the way of things, my kin. Both Graymane and SplitEar wished to rule the Great Pack. Litter-kin though they were, no two kin were less alike than GrayMane and SplitEar. SplitEar was strong and vital. He was the largest and most powerful of the hunting males, and the savage instinct of the FirstBeast rode easily in him. No other of the pack challenged his right to lead the Hunt.

None except his sister GrayMane.

GrayMane didn't have SplitEar's hunting skills. Her nose wasn't as keen to follow the scent of the prey, her eyes weren't as piercing in the darkness under the trees, her body wasn't as large or as powerful.

Still, her soul was like that of a crystalline rock, unbreakable. GrayMane's challenge of SplitEar was a horrible struggle, and many in the Great Pack believed the two would kill each other before one of the two submitted. Their fight on that fateful night lasted from the rising of SmallFace to its setting, and their growling could be heard throughout the lost caves of that first PackHome.

But at last GrayMane realized that she was overmatched. Her brother must win, and so she bared her throat to him. SplitEar howled his triumph to LargeFace as the strongest have always howled, and GrayMane slunk away to lick her terrible wounds. When SplitEar led the hunters out, Gray-Mane stayed behind watching enviously with the pups, the nursing mothers, and others in the pack too weak to hunt.

So it was for two dances of the moons. The Great Pack was a wonder, my kin, even then at the end of its time. The Hunt was a glorious vision, with thousands of kin flowing like quick gray shadows under the trees. PackHome was a vast network of caverns bigger than the forest in which we live now, and each litter mother had her own place within it. The instincts of the SpiritPack drove them, and even without the OldMother's gift of words, the kin had become most favored of all creatures. Of all the beasts of the world, there were none more feared.

Now listen to me, for we come to the crux. The nights of the One Great Pack were passing quickly. The Hunt was failing, even as our hunt fails us now. The kin had become too numerous for the land to support; they had preyed too long in the same area. SplitEar had to lead the Hunt farther and farther from PackHome, and few carriers came back from the Hunt bearing meat for GrayMane and the thousands of others.

The forest then was far more dangerous. Huge Sharp-Fangs, larger and more cunning than the one killed by Silver-Side, lurked in the tree gloom. In times before, they had left the kin alone unless they found a straggler from the Hunt or came on a pup wandering in the forest. But now, with the prey animals killed or driven far away, the SharpFangs had only the kin to eat. Maddened by hunger, they hunted the kin as the kin hunted their own food, not caring for their losses.

A large group of SharpFangs followed the Hunt. During the brightness when the hunters slept, they would attack every day. Without speech, SplitEar and the hunters couldn't act as kin do now, helping each other and coordinating their defense. By the time the third moondance was done, SplitEar had lost a full half of the Hunt and had to return to PackHome.

SplitEar feared that he'd find there only the bones of the rest of the kin. The spirits in him knew that the end had come for the One Pack. The time had come for the Splintering.

During the nights of the long Hunt, GrayMane had done as the OldMother commanded and taught the kin left at Pack-Home the gift of speech. The wisdom of the OldMother was never more needed.

For SplitEar was right. The SharpFangs *did* rage from the forest to attack PackHome, and GrayMane led the kin against them. Armed with words, able to warn each other and arrange their defenses, the kin killed several of the beasts and sent the rest fleeing back into the forest. Though their own losses were still grievous, they survived. The kin praised GrayMane and the OldMother with their new speech.

So it was that when the stragglers of SplitEar's Hunt returned to PackHome at last, they found not bones broken and licked clean of marrow, but the heads of dead SharpFangs hung on poles as warning. GrayMane and the others came out to meet SplitEar. When they saw how few had returned, they howled their lament to the moons.

"How could this have happened?" GrayMane asked Split-Ear. SplitEar could smell the pride in GrayMane, for she had defended PackHome well and knew it. But SplitEar couldn't understand the words GrayMane spoke and so could not reply.

Now, as all kin know, OldMother and FirstBeast have always been at odds, even in the Void. FirstBeast roused a jealousy in SplitEar so that he believed GrayMane was challenging him once more. With a terrible growling, he threatened GrayMane. She cowered back.

"There is no challenge here, SplitEar," she told him. "I beg of you, litter-kin, let us become friends. Let me teach you the OldMother's speech so we can plan for the good of the pack."

The spirit of FirstBeast made SplitEar angrier yet, and he rushed at his sister. She bared her neck immediately to him, but FirstBeast's rage made SplitEar brutal, and he ripped the throat from her.

The earth drank GrayMane's blood as the spirit of Old-Mother wailed.

"All kin are *cursed*!" OldMother cried as her spirit fled from GrayMane. Her fearsome shape hung before the cowering kin, blackening the sky, and her eyes like fire burned them. A raging wind howled and shrieked around her, and dark thunderclouds were her fur.

"The One Pack will now be scattered and diminished. You have thrown away my gift like dumb animals. Now I throw away my protection. You shall howl like the stupid animals you are and not understand one another. Before any kin remembers my gift again, a thousand Great Dances will pass. I will teach others who will listen before you. I tell you, the kin will hear stones speaking before I forgive you."

The AllSpirit heard OldMother's curse and thus it came to be. Those of the kin who had learned to speak were afraid of SplitEar's anger and so remained silent. SplitEar would not lead the kin away from PackHome. The Hunt returned to the forest but found little food, and the SharpFangs returned. SplitEar himself was killed in one such attack, and PackHome was overrun. The beasts cracked the bones of kin and licked them clean. Those who survived fled into the woods—like animals they ran, splitting into small packs of litter-kin.

So it was that the time of the One Pack came to an end.

CHAPTER 6

THE HUNT

"So you think I am GrayMane returned again?" SilverSide said after LifeCrier had finished the tale.

"I do," LifeCrier answered emphatically, still speaking in the formal HuntTongue. "You have come to lead us back to the time of the Great Pack. Can you deny it, SilverSide? Can you say with certainty that I am wrong?"

The robot searched her memory. There was nothing there that directly *contradicted* the possibility, improbable as it might seem. Beyond the moment of her awakening in this place and the erratic store of knowledge she'd been given, there was nothing. Yet . . .

"I can't," SilverSide answered truthfully, as she had to. She shook her head. "I don't know."

"You told me that you were formless as the Void itself when you came. You said that when you saw us, you felt compelled to change your shape so that you looked like us."

"That is true."

"Then what I've said is also true," LifeCrier answered triumphantly, and gave a joyous howl that many of the others joined with. "You've been sent because of the WalkingStones and the Hill of Stars. I know it, SilverSide. I know it as I know the old tales. You're the sign that the OldMother has forgiven us."

SilverSide was troubled. The delicate balance of the Three Laws shifted in her mind, weighing priorities. "Perhaps," she said again. "Possibly. I don't know, LifeCrier. I cannot answer you. I don't know."

SilverSide glanced back at PackHome. KeenEye sat on her haunches at the entrance to the cave, limned in the glow of the moss. The smell of woodfires smoke-preserving the meat in the cold caves was strong in the night. KeenEye stared at SilverSide and the gathering of kin around her, and there was a distinct menace in her gaze. SilverSide knew that if she tried to brush past KeenEye into PackHome, there would be a challenge. Here and now, with no way to back out of it.

First Law imperatives made her turn aside instead, though she hesitated.

With the kin watching, she padded away toward a trail that led to the top of the hill. As she moved away, KeenEye stirred and called after her.

"The Hunt will go out again tomorrow," the leader said in commanding HuntTongue. "You will join us again instead of staying behind at PackHome."

The robot looked back. The Second Law was clear here: KeenEye was a human *and* the leader. "As you wish," she said.

KeenEye nodded. Her eyes glinted, her lips lifted above her incisors. She gave a low BeastTalk growl and settled down in front of the entrance.

SilverSide turned away from the other kin and continued on. She spent the rest of the night alone at the summit of the hill, staring at the moons and the Hill of Stars in the distance. She pondered all that LifeCrier had said and mused over the differences between herself and the kin.

If there was an OldMother, as LifeCrier insisted, She said nothing to SilverSide that night.

KeenEye said nothing to the robot when she came down from the hilltop in the first light of morning.

LifeCrier was as friendly as ever, but the other kin were

less eager than they had been the night before, sensing the unresolved conflict with KeenEye. Where LifeCrier came up to her eagerly, his tongue stroking her face in the greetings of kin, the rest of the wolf-creatures hung back. Though they made way for her as they would have for any higher-status kin, they said very little to her unless she spoke first.

SilverSide's behavior didn't help things. At full light, KeenEye ordered the meat to be dragged from the storage caves for the communal meal. The kin gathered in the largest of the caves, sitting down in a large ragged circle, the pups running in and out among the adults. Smoke-preserved flanks passed from hand to hand.

SilverSide declined her portion.

"I don't eat," she said to the startled adolescent who handed the robot her share. It was only the simple truth—Silverside hadn't even thought it strange. It simply *was*—a fact that somehow she knew. "I cannot even if I wished. It is not necessary for me."

But she heard the BeastTalk grumbling and speculation from some of the others. "You see, KeenEye?" LifeCrier had said. "She is part of the Void, not of the earth. She is full of the spirit of the OldMother."

KeenEye responded with a howl of irritation. "Give her nothing, then, if she insists on playing the OldMother," the leader barked. "And if she hasn't the strength for the Hunt because of it, let the SharpFangs have her." KeenEye growled and stalked from the cave herself, smelling of anger and resentment.

The rest of the day, all the kin but LifeCrier avoided her, though she'd felt them watching and sniffed their uncertainty. Watching and wondering.

The Hunt left PackHome in the early evening, after the heat of the day had subsided and the sunlight turned to evening's gold-green. This time, none of the other kin would place themselves ahead of SilverSide. She was second in the ragged line of kin that trotted down the hill into the green, scent-filled forest.

PackHome was quickly lost behind a screen of foliage and the Hunt was immersed in the sights and scents of the forest.

Birds were beginning to settle in their roosts for the coming night; quick shadows flitting through the branches. Smaller animals scuttled through the underbrush as the pack moved quickly past. KeenEye led them into the glow of the setting sun, and SilverSide wondered at that—the perfect recall of her robotic mind could not forget LifeCrier's remark that the WalkingStones, whatever they were, had driven away the game near the Hill of Stars.

Yet KeenEye padded unerringly in that direction. Once one of the younger kin had questioned KeenEye's path, and the leader had simply turned with a BeastTongue growl that sent the adolescent into submissive silence.

After that, there was no more conversation within the pack at all. They followed KeenEye silently along the winding game trails.

Had SilverSide been human or even kin, she might have marveled at the sights, scents, and sounds of the forest. She might have gaped at the papery pods the size of a youngling dangling from vines and wriggling with some gelatinous interior life. She might have stopped to sniff the perfumed sap oozing up from below a rocky slope. She might have been startled by the shrill rasp of tall weeds that were moving though there was no wind. She might have been captivated by the assorted small animals that leaped across the path or watched as the kin loped quickly by.

Her positronic brain saw it all but without passion. She cared only for that which affected the intricate balance of the Three Laws. She noted that although the small life was abundant, there were few signs of the larger creatures that were food for the kin. She noted the growing apprehension of the pack as KeenEye continued westward.

That resonated with the Laws.

She saw how LifeCrier and the others watched her, waiting to see what the spirit of the OldMother would do, and she wondered if—just maybe—these priorities she felt were a reflection of a goddess's will. Her logic circuits snickered at the thought but couldn't entirely banish the possibility.

The weight of possible danger, tweaking the First Law, nudged SilverSide into speech. She lengthened her stride, moving alongside KeenEye. She used careful KinSpeech, not wanting KeenEye to feel formally challenged. "I've heard LifeCrier and the others say that the meat animals have all left because of the WalkingStones. Is that true, KeenEye?"

"The OldMother didn't bother to tell you?"

"No," the robot answered. Then, when KeenEye said nothing further: "Is it true?" she asked again.

A nod. "You have a problem with that?" KeenEye would not look at her. She continued to trot, her red tongue lolling out between the knives of teeth.

The leader was leaving SilverSide no opening for further questions, forcing the confrontation she was obviously expecting.

SilverSide hesitated. At last she dropped back into the pack again.

They continued on.

By midnight, the pack was very near where the Hill of Stars had glowed the night before. There was an odd silence in the woods, as if most of the creatures that normally lived here had gone. The very silence nudged SilverSide again.

She did what none of the kin would have dared to do. The decision was simple; the reasoning complex.

By deliberately failing to define "human," by not even telling the robot that it *was* a robot, Janet Anastasi had forced upon her robot an unusual freedom of action and a liberal interpretation of the Three Laws. She'd made a construct that didn't consider itself mechanical.

She would likely have been pleased with what the robot had done so far, with SilverSide's "creativity."

But SilverSide was still bound to the Laws. The Second Law demanded that she obey humans, and she had accepted the wolf-creatures as "human." In a pack society, the leader spoke for all; therefore, KeenEye's commands must carry more weight than that of any of the other kin.

Yet the First Law demanded that she protect human life, and logic led her to favor the many over the few. If KeenEye was indeed leading the pack into danger, the First Law demanded action. Yet she'd already seen that the very lifestyle of the kin involved danger—the SharpFangs, the leadership challenges within the pack, the scarcity of food. One could not be "human" and avoid danger. That damped the strength of the First Law.

She had to know more. She might not be forced to action, but she *was* compelled to ask.

She ran swiftly in front of the leader. For a moment, SilverSide thought that KeenEye would simply ignore her and shoulder past, and the balance within her shifted again. But KeenEye drew up short. The pack came to a ragged halt behind KeenEye. SilverSide could smell their anticipation.

"If the kin need food, what good does it do us to go west?" She used HuntTongue, stressing the importance of her question.

KeenEye gave her only a low BeastTalk rumble deep in her throat. She glared and sat back on her hind legs, the clawed forepaws threateningly ready.

KeenEye was not going to answer the question, SilverSide realized. But then LifeCrier pushed his grizzled muzzle forward and yapped support. "SilverSide asks the question we all have, KeenEye."

KeenEye looked back at the line of kin. They were staring back, quiet and very intent. SilverSide knew that the leader saw the subliminal challenge there. Most of the kin had gathered around LifeCrier, saying nothing but lending their unvoiced support to his question.

Frost blue eyes turned back to SilverSide. "Do you challenge me now, SilverSide? Is that what the OldMother tells you?" she asked.

"There is no food," SilverSide said. "The forest here is empty of all the meat animals. That's why I spoke."

"You don't even eat the meat. Why should you care?"

SilverSide searched within her mind. "I must do what is best for all kin."

"That is the *leader's* task." KeenEye growled for emphasis. "*Only* the leader's task."

Balances changed again.

The robot had no doubt that it was more intelligent than any of the kin. She *knew* things, whether inborn memory or the OldMother's gift. She could see a hundred ways to improve the life of the kin. She was also physically stronger than any of them, and she could change her shape if need be.

More intelligent. Stronger. The chosen of the OldMother. All that, coupled with KeenEye's insistence on coming here, spoke through the Laws.

The decision clicked in her mind, firm and certain. Silver-Side could best obey the laws in her head by leading the pack.

"I challenge you, KeenEye," SilverSide said in Hunt-Tongue.

KeenEye seemed to sigh. Her eyes closed as if in momentary prayer. "As you wish," she said.

The wolf-creature came at SilverSide in a snarling rush, her jaws wide open to rip at the robot's throat. But SilverSide, with the superb reflexes Janet Anastasi had given her, was no longer there. She moved back on her hind feet and turned, sliding aside just enough so that KeenEye's momentum took her past her. Silverside reached out and shoved KeenEye as she tried to turn. KeenEye nearly crashed headlong into a tree, falling and rolling hard. The leader bounded to her feet quickly, but there was a dazed glassiness in her eyes.

KeenEye stood two-legged, howled at SilverSide, and leaped, fingers out to claw the robot.

This time SilverSide allowed KeenEye to strike her. Claws scraped on her metal flanks without leaving a mark. KeenEye howled in anger, frustration, and pain, and raked at SilverSide again, trying for the eyes. They were vulnerable, if her skin was not. SilverSide flinched.

Rearing back, SilverSide blocked the curving blow and grabbed KeenEye's hand/paw, twisting the joint. KeenEye screeched, though SilverSide was careful not to break any bones. Slowly, she forced the wrist backward—as KeenEye thrashed to get free, as she spat at the robot, as she clawed with her free hand. Nothing she did seemed to hurt the robot. SilverSide was far too strong for the wolf-creature.

SilverSide forced KeenEye down to the grass and pulled her over on her back.

"Submit," she whispered to the leader, and it seemed the others heard an odd sympathy in her voice. She did not seem happy in her victory.

"Kill me," KeenEye grunted back, her lips bared over her fangs. She snapped uselessly at SilverSide. "I will not submit. Kill me."

SilverSide put more pressure on the hold. Ligaments groaned. "Submit," she said again. "I need you to help me, and you are useless to the pack dead. Give me your throat."

The defiance went out of KeenEye. The paw was limp in SilverSide's grasp. KeenEye tilted her muzzle back in submission.

Yet even as SilverSide stood in triumph over KeenEye, there was a crashing of underbrush behind her and a screech of pain from one of the kin.

First Law reaction whirled SilverSide around as a youngling was hurled through the air to fall near SilverSide. He rolled on the ground bleeding from a deep gash in his side and yelping in pain.

"A WalkingStone!" LifeCrier shouted. "Beware!"

SilverSide's lips drew back in a BeastTongue snarl.

Standing over the wounded kin was the apparition that had just burst through the trees. It stood on two legs, its hands clenched into fists encased in a shiny metal skin. It was far larger than any of the kin, and if what it had done to the youngling was an indication, it was immensely strong. Behind the featureless head, SilverSide could hear motors whirring softly.

It smelled of lightning and stone.

The head swiveled. The apparition seemed to regard SilverSide strangely.

Then, with a swiftness that surprised her, it charged!

The pack was milling in confusion. LifeCrier howled a lament for the downed youngling as those in the direct path of the WalkingStone scattered. Only SilverSide was immune to the panic.

She could only respond as the Laws allowed her, and the First Law left her no choice.

She lunged forward, slamming herself hard into the chest of the constructed *thing* that had attacked the kin without warning. There was no hesitation to her action at all—it was a pure First Law response to protect the life of "humans."

Her jaws closed on an unyielding metallic arm; with a strength equal to her own, the WalkingStone flung SilverSide away. She rolled to soften the impact, allowing her body to deform to absorb the shock.

She whirled back to attack.

LifeCrier and KeenEye had rallied the others. All but the carriers tethered to the *travois* formed a ragged circle around the injured youngling, protecting him from the WalkingStone. They snarled and snapped, making quick thrusts of their own but staying out of range of the powerful arms.

The WalkingStone had stopped, pointing a finger at the

pack. SilverSide, in motion, saw the fingertip become round and a dark opening appear at its apex.

Weapon! The word screamed in SilverSide's head.

"KeenEye!" she shouted. "Scatter!"

She hurled herself at the WalkingStone's extended arm.

Metal clashed against metal. A line of searing, intense light cut a crazy swath harmlessly through foliage as Silverside's rush knocked the WalkingStone's arm aside. The kin yelped and retreated again.

Gears whirred menacingly inside the WalkingStone. The smell of it made SilverSide snarl. The featureless, impassive face turned toward SilverSide, who faced it defiantly. Deliberately, the WalkingStone pointed its deadly, laser-tipped finger at her. The aiming beam tracked brilliant red across her body; the skin glowed white just behind. The ferocious heat translated as pain to SilverSide's positronic brain; the "human" responses overlaid there made her yelp in response though the tough metal alloy was only scorched, not yet melted. Still, the attack disrupted circuitry to that side of her body.

She went down.

The WalkingStone turned its attention back to the pack, now huddled in a knot around the youngling "SilverSide?" LifeCrier called, her fear-scent strong. "What do we do?"

SilverSide tried to answer. Nothing happened. Her vocal circuits were temporarily gone as well.

KeenEye and LifeCrier tried to rally the kin.

The pack had its own peculiar method of fighting, as SilverSide had seen before on their way from her Egg to PackHome. She knew what KeenEye's command barks said.

"Circle. Keep moving. Keep the WalkingStone busy, but don't let it touch you." A SharpFang would have been dealt with in much the same way, the pack whirling around it like a clawing, biting tornado, dashing in behind to nip at ankles and then leaping back, harrying the creature until—exhausted and frustrated—it gave them a fatal opening. Then they would swarm in as one and bear it down.

Such tactics gave the kin the ability to deal with carnivores far larger and stronger than themselves.

Such tactics were horribly ill-suited for their current foe.

It required no effort for SilverSide to picture what would happen if the WalkingStone used its laser on any of the kin. The urgent First Law need to respond drove everything else from SilverSide's mind.

With the left side of her body still shut down, there was only one possibility. With *anything* fashioned to resemble a living creature, the joints—neck, elbows, knees—are the most fragile area. SilverSide knew that: as a shapechanger herself, structural dynamics were part of her core knowledge. Her malleable body shifted, altered. The mostly immobile left side she rounded as best she could; everything else she metamorphosed into a massive, coiled muscle.

She gathered herself. Aimed.

Leapt.

Metal boomed against metal like a thunderclap.

The WalkingStone's neck was stabilized with supports, but none were designed to withstand the tremendous hammer blow SilverSide represented. There was a screech and a wail of stressed steel. Welds popped as the head was suddenly canted at an acute angle. The glowing eyes dimmed. The thing staggered, the laser fired wildly and high. Its knees buckled, it seemed to wheeze mechanically.

It fell.

As it fell, SilverSide heard its voice in her head. Oddly, SilverSide understood it, for the thing spoke in the language she'd been born with. *Central, under attack, badly damaged and shutting down. . . .* The voice trailed off. None of the kin looked as if they'd heard it.

SilverSide had fallen herself, resuming her wolf shape. As her body cooled, control returned. She managed to limp slowly to her feet, and stood on her hind legs over the fallen WalkingStone. It twitched spasmodically, but seemed no threat. Its mental voice was silent. As SilverSide watched, a plume of thin, acrid smoke came from the broken neck, and all movement stopped.

SilverSide lifted her muzzle and gave a BeastTalk howl of triumph as she'd seen the other kin do after a kill. The others howled with her.

LifeCrier and KeenEye padded over. Both groveled in

front of SilverSide, baring their necks in ritual submission.
"You are the Bane of WalkingStones," LifeCrier declared.
"You saved our lives and the lives of all the kin here."

"Yes," SilverSide answered. It was not immodesty; it was
simply truth.

KeenEye rose, her eyes unreadable. "I was wrong," she
said. "What LifeCrier said of you is true. You are the wisest of
us. You are the OldMother's gift." She paused "You are now
the leader of kin."

"Yes," SilverSide said.

The decision echoed in all her judgment circuits. "Yes, I
am," she repeated.

CHAPTER 8

A HURRIED DEPARTURE

The hard thing under his cheek seemed to be a foot. It was attached to a very smooth and shapely leg, and at the top of the leg . . .

"Derec," a woman's sleepy contralto said warningly from farther down the bed. A warm breath tickled his shin. "I'm very, very cross when rudely awakened."

"You don't like it?"

Ariel wriggled under his attention. "It's not . . ." she breathed, then sighed. "I'm just tired."

"Too tired?"

She gasped. "Oh, you . . ." In a flurry of bedcovers, she whirled around. Her mouth touched his. She rolled him on his back.

Much later, they snuggled together. Derec reached out from the cover to touch the contact that caused the wall of the bedroom to become one-way transparent. Though in the middle of Aurora's largest city, there was nothing to be seen but green, open expanse. They looked out over an expanse of a lush rolling meadow, crowned with a stand of magnificent trees. The orange-red sun of Aurora slashed through the branches, wedges of light outlined in a miasma of morning fog.

A native whose whole life had been spent on the planet might have shrugged—beautiful Auroran sunrises were commonplace enough to have become the norm—but in the year since Derec and Ariel had been on the planet, they hadn't yet become blasé. They gazed at the display as if the awakening world had arranged it strictly for their benefit.

"It's very lovely," Ariel whispered.

"Like you."

"Flatterer."

"Will it get me anywhere?"

"We'll see. Maybe. A little later, anyway."

"There's no reason to wait."

"Greedy this morning, aren't we? Well, you'll just have to cultivate a little patience."

Ariel kissed him again and rolled from the bed. With a lithe grace, she moved across the room. She'd recovered entirely from her ordeal in Robot City, or at least it seemed that way. The disease that had warped her personality had been cured, her injuries healed. She had left Robot City and returned to normal.

But not Derec. The chemfets—tiny viral replicas of the Robot City material developed by his father, Dr. Avery—had been implanted in Derec. Though he'd gained control of the chemfets after they'd threatened to take him over, the ordeal had left him permanently linked to the city. Even now he could, if he wished, listen to the inner conversations in his body and hear the sounds of the Robot City central computer, across light-years of distance. He could give the city orders, direct the actions of its myriad robots, alter its programming. . . .

Derec did not enjoy playing god, no matter how minor a one. He didn't enjoy being shackled to his father's mad creation. He especially didn't enjoy the fact that he didn't yet know the full extent of that inner universe.

They were still chained to Avery, even now. Their return to Aurora and the tale of Robot City had made news everywhere on that world. They were celebrities. Even now, they could not go out in the public areas of the city without someone coming up to them.

The thoughts drove away his good humor. He looked out at

the Auroran dawn and suddenly saw nothing. The dawn might as well have been a computerized image projected on a wall. He sighed.

"I know that look," Ariel said from the open door of the personal. "You're brooding again."

"No, I'm not."

"You are too. I've been with you too long not to know. You're thinking about Robot City again."

There was an edge to her voice that made Derec grimace. Theirs had been a roller-coaster ride of a relationship: they never seemed to be able to settle into any semblance of normalcy. When things were good, they were very good indeed. And when they were bad . . .

That was Avery's legacy as well—many of the memories Derec and Ariel shared were not pleasant. For the months they'd been trapped in Robot City, Ariel's personality had been in a steady, disintegrating spiral, fluctuating between vivacious and darkly sullen.

At least she'd escaped. At least she'd escaped from that planet and been cured.

Derec could never leave Robot City. It would always be there within him. It was his, his responsibility, whether he wanted it or not.

"Derec, stop it," Ariel said warningly.

"Stop what?"

"I'm not going to answer something that obvious. Figure it out yourself."

He knew he should have apologized then. He knew he should have smiled deprecatingly and shrugged, should have risen himself and kissed her until she forgot the argument and the dawn was again something beautiful to see.

But he didn't.

"Sorry I'm so stupid," he said bitterly.

Ariel's face was red with irritation, her eyes narrowed and her hands clenched into angry fists. "Derec, don't spoil the morning, please."

"*I'm* not the one who knows what everyone else is thinking. It seems to me that you claimed that ability. *I* thought everything was going fine."

"You're being childish."

"And you're being arrogant."

"Arrogant? Damn it, Derec...Derec?" She stopped. Derec was no longer listening to her. He was standing in the middle of the room, his gaze inward and blind.

The call had entered Derec's mind with an urgency that was almost painful. Aurora, the dawn outside the window, Ariel's voice: they'd all disappeared in the frantic *need* of the message. The chemfets relayed the message to him.

Under attack, it said. The call was faint, as if coming from a great distance, much farther than the Robot City he knew. *Request immediate help*.

"What is it, Derec?" Ariel asked again, a look of concern furrowing her brow. Her anger was lost in her worry for him. Slowly, he came back to an awareness of the room around him.

"I'm . . . I'm not sure." He was still holding his head with a look of inward concentration, listening to those whispering pleas only he could hear. "It's the chemfets again. I'm . . . I'm getting a series of coordinates and a distress signal from a source claiming to be the central computer. It says it's Robot City, but—Mandlebrot!" he called suddenly.

The robot slipped quickly from a niche on one side of the bedroom. Derec had assembled the robot from assorted parts, a hodgepodge of models including a right arm constructed of what he called Avery material—infinitely malleable and adjustable. The patchwork-quilt effect lent the robot, to say the least, a unique look, and Derec had a vast affection for him.

"Mandelbrot, you're also linked to Robot City," he said to the robot. "Did you just receive a distress call?"

"No, Master Derec, I did not."

"If I give you a set of coordinates, can you tell me whether they're anywhere near Robot City?"

"I can link with the Auroran Net and access records there."

"Good." Derec rattled off the coordinates he'd heard in his head. Mandelbrot stood silently a moment, then spoke.

"Those coordinates are for a region well outside human space and distant from Robot City, though in the same arm of the galaxy. If I have not received the message you received, and if those coordinates represent the actual source of the call, then I can see two possibilities: first, that Dr. Avery himself has established a new Robot City somewhere, perhaps by using the Keys of Perihelion to jump to another world. Or, secondly, that the distress call is from a Robot City that is an offshoot of the original. We know that some of the Avery robots were sent out by the central computer to start new sites on other planets. Can you communicate with the computer yourself?"

Derec concentrated, but the wispy tendrils of the repeating call were gone as if they had never been there. "No," he said. "There's nothing now."

"There's a third, even more likely, possibility you've both missed," Ariel said, hands on hips. "It was your imagination. You've done nothing but worry about Robot City since we left."

"It wasn't my imagination," Derec insisted. "It was real. I know the difference, Ariel."

"You said it was faint."

"It came through the chemfets. I can guarantee that."

"All right," Ariel sighed. "All right. I'm tired of arguing. It's gone now, so let's forget it. Mandelbrot, you can go back to the niche."

As Mandelbrot turned obediently, Derec shook his head. "No. I can't just forget it, Ariel. It's not that simple. You don't seem to realize that, to a large extent, I *am* Robot City now. I'm part of it; I'm responsible."

Ariel whirled around at that, her face angry. Her finger dug into his chest, prodding.

"*No*. No, you're not, Derec. Your father's responsible. Avery. Without his poisoning you with the chemfets, without his interference and his insane schemes, none of this would have happened—to *any* of us. You're not responsible, Derec, any more than I am or Mandelbrot is or Wolruf is. You can't blame yourself for any of it, and there's nothing you can do about it."

"There's trouble," Derec insisted. "I can feel it. I have to go see. Mandelbrot, I want you to see that our ship is provisioned and ready to go by noon."

Mandelbrot hesitated, caught for a second between the conflicting orders, but Derec was his primary master. His orders took precedence over Ariel's. The robot nodded and moved to the computer terminal on the wall. Mandelbrot activated the screen and opened a line to the Aurora Port computer.

Ariel shook her head, dark hair swaying with savage motion. She jabbed at Derec's chest again with the forefinger. "You're not doing it, Derec. No. If this phantom city in your mind has problems, then let it deal with them on its own. That's what the central computer is for. And if it's Avery again, if he's used his Keys to jump from Robot City to some other place he's set up, it'll be a trap just like the other. I'm not at all interested in stepping into his deadly little webs again."

"I don't want you to. I wasn't intending to have you go along. I thought just Mandelbrot and myself . . ."

The words didn't come out quite as he'd intended. *Because I don't want you to get hurt again,* he should have added. *Because I care too much about you.* But her face was already clouded, and somehow the words wouldn't come now.

Ariel nodded, muscles bunched as she set her jaw. "Fine," she said, her words clipped and short. "Just fine. I'm sorry I'm such a burden."

"Ariel . . ."

But she was no longer listening. She went to her closet, snatched a loose smock from a hook, and tugged it on. She brushed her fingers through her hair and gave Derec one last smouldering gaze.

Then she stalked from the house.

"Mandelbrot," Derec said after the reverberations of her exit had stopped echoing through the house. "You should be glad that you don't have to deal with emotions."

"It has been my observation that human feelings are much like fruit."

"Hmm? I'm not sure I understand."

"If handled roughly, both feelings and fruit are easily bruised."

To that, Derec didn't have a reply.

CHAPTER 9

THE HILL OF STARS

SilverSide knew the normal pack routine with a kill.

The hunters would first tear open the abdomen and feed themselves on the warm, pulsing blood-rich meat. Afterward, their own appetites sated, they would use their crude flint-knapped knives and flay the carcass, cutting it into manageable chunks to be put on the carriers.

Now the kin circled uneasily around the dead Walking-Stone. LifeCrier reached out and tapped at the thing's stomach with a claw. "It's stone, SilverSide," the old wolf-creature said. "A magical creature from the FirstBeast. There's nothing for us to eat. It's a mockery."

SilverSide came up to the body, the other kin moving aside for her. "KeenEye," she asked, "have any of the Walking-Stones been killed before?"

KeenEye seemed grateful for the attention, as SilverSide had expected. "No," she said. "These are the Hunters of the WalkingStones; there are other kinds near the Hill of Stars, but they never leave that place. Every time before, we ran from the Hunters when we couldn't hurt them. They've killed three hands of kin and more in the three dances of the moons since they came. The fire from their fingers kills."

Three hands of kin—with the wolf-creature's four-fingered hands, that meant that over a dozen kin had fallen to the Walking-Stones in three months. SilverSide had seen perhaps thirty to forty of the wolf-creatures at PackHome. Twelve members of the tribe was a significant loss. It was no wonder that LifeCrier and the others were looking for divine intervention.

SilverSide crouched down alongside the WalkingStone. She examined the thing carefully. Her optical circuits noted a seam running along the abdomen. She slid a clawtip carefully along the edge, narrowing and flattening the claw so that it slipped easily under the lip of metal.

She pried up. Magnetic catches held tenaciously, then finally gave as she increased the tension. The abdomen covering lifted, revealing an interior of miniature servo motors, linkages, wires, and circuit boards. The kin around SilverSide gasped.

"There's no blood," KeenEye said in SilverSide's ear, marveling. "No muscles, no meat, no stomach. How does it move?"

"Magic," LifeCrier said again. "The Eternal Ones have set them in motion against SilverSide and the OldMother."

The answer sounded right to SilverSide. She could not refute LifeCrier, not with the strange gaps in her knowledge. LifeCrier had told her of the struggles among the gods. SilverSide had found nothing to disprove that she had been sent by the OldMother to serve humans. Given that, it was just as likely that the WalkingStones may well have been sent by FirstBeast or some other rival of the OldMother.

Still . . .

"The Hunter is not magic," SilverSide told them. "The WalkingStones are MadeThings. They are tools, like our flint knives or the *travois*. They are like the dolls the cubs fashion from sticks, only the WalkingStones are stuffed with stone chips and vines from the Void. The power in them allows them to walk, and they speak with a voice you can hear only in your head.

"Look," she said and plunged her forepaw hand into the WalkingStone's entrails. Her claws emerged again fisted around the colorful intestines of the creature: a trailing, knotted coil of wires. The kin howled at the sight, half in lament, half in wonder.

"These are the guts of kin's worst enemy," SilverSide said. "The cubs back at PackHome could at least eat a SharpFang. Even if SharpFangs kill kin, they can also feed us. But not these creatures. This is the inedible meat of the Walking-Stones."

"What are we going to do, SilverSide?" LifeCrier asked, and his question was echoed by the others around them.

SilverSide thought for a moment. Then she tugged hard at the array of wires. Bright sparks spat angrily, arcing and dying on the ground. SilverSide flung the tangle down.

"Since they will not let us live, we will kill them," she said.

A robotics expert would probably have been simply appalled and frightened and ordered the destruction of the robot. Janet Anastasi, SilverSide's creator, might have herself been concerned with the robot's behavior, but she would have also been intensely interested.

SilverSide's mindset had nothing of a human being in it at all. The Three Laws were there, yes, but they had now been completely reshaped and changed. As the robots of Aurora, Solaria, Earth, and other human worlds were shaped and designed to mimic human behavior, so SilverSide had shaped and designed herself to mimic the kin. Indeed, because she had no conception that she was a constructed thing herself, she *was* kin, and she interpreted the inbuilt Three Laws of her positronic brain in light of her own "humanity."

The WalkingStones threatened the Kin. They killed kin. And though she could have led the kin away from PackHome, that also would have meant the probable loss of life. The wolf-creatures were territorial hunters, and the neighboring pack-leaders had already warned them. SilverSide's pack couldn't move into another pack's territory without being challenged and having to fight other wolf-creatures, nor would another pack have allowed them to hunt in their own territory.

Finding another viable home that was not already claimed was at best a dubious hope, and KeenEye and LifeCrier had already told her that the WalkingStones were expanding their holdings—even if SilverSide's pack left, another pack would eventually have to confront the WalkingStones when they might be even more powerful.

SilverSide had reluctantly come to the decision to stay and confront the situation directly.

Yes, kin might die, but *more* kin would likely die if they left.

A human robot might have looked for yet another, more peaceful solution. But SilverSide was a carnivore, a hunter even though she herself did not eat at all; she took the carnivore's solution.

Having accepted the wolf-creatures as human, she accepted their mores. Without further proof, she also accepted their mythology. The OldMother had sent her. She was *chosen* for the task. The WalkingStones might be intelligent, but they were made by another god and therefore were not "human" themselves. Though SilverSide couldn't perform outside the Three Laws, she would do what she had to do within their limits.

As her new mindset perceived them.

What the carnivore could not avoid, it attacked. Dr. Anastasi's experiment had worked perfectly well. Her robot had become something *other*. A very dangerous other.

Still, if it weren't for the fact that SilverSide had just killed one of the hated creatures, the rest of the kin might not have accepted her statement. A challenge to her leadership might have been the immediate outcome.

Even so, there were questions.

"We've tried killing the WalkingStones before," KeenEye said. She used KinSpeech rather than HuntTongue, not wanting SilverSide to think she was offering formal challenge. SilverSide listened to the old leader, sitting back on her hind legs and braiding a necklace from the WalkingStone's wires. "They're not like SharpFangs. SharpFangs are strong but very stupid. These Hunter WalkingStones can kill by pointing their fingers, and our claws and teeth do nothing.

"This one died," SilverSide said. She placed the necklace

around her neck; the other kin howled softly at the sight.

"Yes, but it's the first."

"It won't be the last. I will show you ways to deal with them. This is *our* territory, not the WalkingStones'. They are driving away the game we live on and making this a barren place. Once the WalkingStones and their Hill of Stars are gone, the game will return and the kin can live as they please. We will take our territory back again."

"You will show us how to kill them?"

"I will."

KeenEye paused. She looked from the dead WalkingStone to SilverSide. "Then lead us, SilverSide," KeenEye said in a rising shout and let out a glad cry in BeastTalk.

SilverSide took a strand of wires from the gutted Hunter. She quickly plaited another necklace from the colorful wire and knotted the bright coil around KeenEye's neck. Carefully, she then did the same with each of them. "There," she said when it was done. "We wear the signs of our victory. Now, follow me. We must learn more about our enemy."

SilverSide dropped to all fours. With a quick lope, she ran into the forest, moving westward toward the Hill of Stars.

Howling, the rest of the kin ran behind her.

CHAPTER 10
AN UNEXPECTED MESSAGE, AN UNEXPECTED ARRIVAL

"Katherine Ariel Burgess, you're a fool."

The image in the mirror didn't seem inclined to answer the accusation. Ariel scowled at herself and slapped at the contact. The mirror dissolved in a shimmering crystalline haze and was replaced by a pastoral sunset scene. That only made her more angry, reminding her of the acrimonious morning a week ago.

She'd told herself that Derec would wait, that he'd still be there when she came back from her long walk. But he hadn't waited.

When she'd finally cooled down and called the house in mid-afternoon, Balzac, the household robot, had informed her that Derec and Mandelbrot had left for the port several hours before. Ariel had called the port, wondering what she'd say if he was still there, rehearsing the lines in her mind.

I've changed my mind, Derec. I want to go with you.

But he'd already gone, and she had no idea where it was he was heading.

Ariel didn't know whether that made her angry or sad or both at the same time. She simply felt confused. The intervening days hadn't made things any better. Sleeping alone each night was too vivid a reminder.

She came out of the personal, wandering aimlessly through rooms that now seemed far too large and empty. She stared out the windows, fiddled with the reader, flicked on the holovid and as quickly turned if off again.

With a start, she noticed that the computer terminal was blinking. Feeling a sudden surge of hope, she started to press the access key. Stopped.

"Balzac?" she called.

The robot trundled from its wall niche in the next room. "Mistress?" it said in a flat, mechanical voice. Balzac was a utility model, unsophisticated and plain.

"The message on the terminal. Why didn't you answer the call?"

"I monitored the message, but it was for Derec and did not demand a reply."

"Who was it from?"

"'Who' is imprecise in this case. The message was a faint relay from a central computer system."

Ariel's lips pressed together. She inhaled slowly, thinking. "Thank you, Balzac. That's all I require."

The robot nodded and left the room. Ariel waited until it was gone and the house was silent again, then spoke her codeword to the terminal: "Euler"—the name of one of the supervisor robots on Robot City. Nothing happened. She wrinkled her nose.

She knew Derec's codeword as well; he'd made no attempt to keep it a secret from her. "Aranimas," she said.

A foil screen scrolled open; glowing letters flickered across it as Ariel leaned closer. The message was short and succinct:

CITY UNDER ATTACK BY NON-HUMANS. IMPERATIVE WE RECEIVE OUTSIDE AID.

The message was followed by a sequence of coordinate numbers for the location. Ariel smiled. "Okay, Derec," she said to the screen. "If the mountain has run away from Mohammed, Mohammed will chase it. Won't you be surprised when I show up?"

She turned away from the computer, suddenly excited. This would serve him right. "Balzac!" she called. "I need you to make some arrangements."

"Mandelbrot, the Robot City has to be somewhere on that large continent there—see where the two rivers meet in the forested area? The computer says that's where the last message was 'waved from."

Mandelbrot, at the controls of their craft, punched in coordinates. "Have you been able to get the city's central computer to respond?"

"No," Derec admitted glumly. "Either I'm not doing something right or the chemfets only give me access to the original Robot City's computer. Before, all I had to do was *think* a message and it went through. This Central won't talk to me or the original Robot City's computer. It's just beaming out the distress call at regular intervals."

"Then it must be expecting someone to answer; otherwise, why signal at all?"

"I don't know, I don't know. I haven't figured it out yet. I'm just as puzzled as you are."

Derec watched the long curve of the world flatten as they approached. It was a pretty world, he decided. He might have chosen it himself. It seemed a calm and gentle place, much like Aurora, though he could see the spiraling arms of a storm just touching the eastern shores of the continent below, and he knew that underneath the pastel blue-white would be dark, streaking clouds and raging winds.

Untamed, this world was. Which was very *unlike* Aurora.
And very much like Ariel.

The thought crossed his mind, unbidden. She'd not sent any messages to him after she'd stormed out of the house; in fact, she'd disappeared entirely. He'd made calls to a few places trying to find her before they'd left, but to no avail. She seemed to have dropped from sight. It had been very hard to leave without saying goodbye. And because he knew that was exactly the effect she'd been after, he'd gone.

He'd begun to wonder if she'd be there when he came

back. There was a sullen ache in him at the image of an empty house. It was going to hurt. It was going to hurt more than he wanted to think about.

To take his mind off Ariel, he reached in front of Mandelbrot and toggled a switch to bring the world into closer focus. Unbroken treetops swayed in a light wind.

"I don't see any evidence of a city," he said. "If we weren't looking specifically for it because of the signal, I'd swear this place was barren of any technology. It has to be there, though. If so, it sure hasn't spread out as much as the original. Have you seen any evidence of other life, Mandelbrot?"

"No, Derec. The nightside umbra shows no obvious large habitations, which would be lighted, I would think—though we haven't seen this continent at night yet. The atmospheric sampling does indicate a small amount of industrial waste, which is very likely the result of your city. You remember the effect the other one had on its environment."

Derec did. The massive, out-of-control building spree of the first Robot City had resulted in immense ecological side effects. The horrendous deluges that daily inundated the city had nearly killed both him and Ariel until he'd reprogrammed the central computer. "Yes, I remember," he said. "I hope this one keeps a better handle on things. Take us down. Let's see what's going on."

"Derec, I advise against landing in the city itself. Assuming we can even find it."

"Why not, Mandelbrot?"

The robot's eyes gleamed as it turned to him. "We do not know what kind of attack this city is facing," he said. "I have checked for other ships in orbit and found nothing, but I am still concerned that a city under attack will have defenses against ships. You cannot communicate with the central computer. Given that, I would be afraid that it might deem an unidentified ship an enemy and take measures to protect itself."

Derec grimaced.

"If you order me to do so," Mandelbrot continued, "I will trust your better judgment and follow your orders."

Derec shook his head. "Uh-uh. And you'll say 'I told you so' afterward."

"No." The flat delivery almost sounded hurt.

"Okay," Derec said, grinning. "I think you're right. Let's land elsewhere. How much of a hike were you planning on giving us?"

"I have estimated that fifty kilometers is the minimum."

"Fine. A few days' stroll through the forest—"

At that moment, the craft shook like a mad thing. As the hull shuddered, Derec felt Mandelbrot's firm grip on his arm, guiding him to his seat and forcing him down. The crash webbing slid over him as the craft tumbled; Mandelbrot staggered back to his seat and fought the controls.

"What happened?" Derec shouted.

"I do not know. Our orbit is decaying rapidly. . . ." The robot had no time to say more as the ship's view of the world below spun and whirled. Mandelbrot's robotic reflexes were far faster than Derec's, but the power to their main engines was simply gone.

Using the attitude jets, Mandelbrot managed to reduce the wild tumbling momentarily, but then the first tendrils of the atmosphere touched them and the hull struts moaned in agony. The ship began to do gymnastics again, and this time—snared in the planet's gravity well—they were flung violently with it.

Derec's head slammed up against his seat despite the webbing, making him shout in pain. Mandelbrot had cut all the automatics, giving him full control of the ship, but it was of little help. In the viewscreen, they saw the hull turning cherry red; the heat was suffocating in the cabin, the ventilation system gone.

White cloudtops seemed to race toward them, then they plunged into the columns of gray murk. Storm winds tossed them; rain sheeted across the screen.

"Mandelbrot!" Derec's scream shivered with the vibrations of the ship.

There was no answer.

They plunged out of the bottom of the storm, the murky landscape below wheeling like a mad carousel. The ground, a fist waiting to crumple them like paper, rushed at them.

Then, like the gut-wrenching end of a roller-coaster's free-fall, Derec was shoved down in his seat as the craft pulled up in a quick loop.

For a moment, Derec thought Mandelbrot had saved them.

It was still too late.

The trailing bulk of the engines caught the lip of a rocky outcropping. The granite blade of the hill ripped into the supports. Metal and stone screeched; Derec heard the concussion as the engine exploded. Snared, the ship itself was hammered to the ground. The inferno of the engine was sheared completely off and went spiraling away.

At least I won't burn to death.

As a last thought, it seemed a strange comfort.

CHAPTER 11

STRATEGY AND TACTICS

SilverSide brought the pack to a ragged halt at a ridge looking down into the shallow bowl of a valley perhaps a kilometer across at its widest point. She sat in the shadows of the last few trees; LifeCrier and KeenEye came forward and sat on their haunches to either side of the new leader. SmallFace was high in the sky; LargeFace had yet to rise. The stars—the VoidEyes, as LifeCrier called them—stared down at the city and marveled.

SilverSide felt some of that awe herself. The Hill of Stars, set like a glistening diamond in the center of the valley and rising well above the level of the surrounding hills, was a fantastic pattern of glowing lights. The slender pyramidal structure mocked the glory of the night sky.

Nor was the Hill of Stars all. Other buildings spread out around it in geometric splendor, a procession of hard, crystalline shapes filling the valley and spilling out its open end, all linked by ribbons of walkways.

And everywhere, *everywhere,* there were WalkingStones: all different sizes, all different builds, all different colors. They bustled along the walkways, gazed from the windows of the buildings, slid busily between the flanks of the city. There were thousands of them.

They moved in an eerie, almost mystical silence—at least to the kin. But SilverSide could hear the deafening roar of the city's voices inside her head. An eternal chatter of orders and instructions came from the central computer; reports were constantly being funneled back to that source. And she understood the words, for they spoke as the Hunter spoke, in that language SilverSide guessed must be that of the Void where the gods lived. It was more proof that the OldMother was being opposed.

"They began with just the Hill of Stars," KeenEye whispered to SilverSide. She panted at the remembrance, and her long, furless tail lashed from side to side. "They've worked like the *krajal* since then."

SilverSide had seen the industrious insects called the *krajal* toiling ceaselessly through the undergrowth of the forest, building their mud colonies on the sides of trees. KeenEye pointed a long finger at the periphery of the city, her lips drawn back from canines in a snarl.

"See how they tear down the trees and destroy the land?" she rasped. "All this valley was forest before the Walking-Stones came. They destroy everything to put up their stone caves. And the light—it's as if the sun were resting down there for the night. The WalkingStones don't care about kin or any of the living creatures. They don't care that our prey animals have fled. They don't care that their stone caves stretch out and out and out. Long before they reach PackHome, we will have left. We will have starved, or we will have been killed."

"Do these other WalkingStones hurt the kin like the one we killed?" SilverSide asked. "There must be different *species* of WalkingStones down there."

"We don't know," KeenEye answered. "The others have never bothered us. They stay within the stones. Only the Hunters ever come outside."

"That also makes them like the *krajal*," LifeCrier added. "Only the blue *krajali* get food, only the yellow-speckled *krajali* build the tree-homes; only the red *krajali* defend the homes against the LongTongues. They each have a separate task to do, and they each are shaped a little differently. Maybe it's the same with these WalkingStones."

SilverSide's optics focused more closely on the hive of activity. What LifeCrier had said sounded like an accurate enough metaphor. The view of the city bore that out. Certainly the WalkingStones seemed specialized in appearance. And though the WalkingStones were obviously constructed things, their hard, unyielding bodies were like the chitinous shells of insects.

Maybe the enemy of the OldMother had fashioned the WalkingStones after insects. They had the same outward silence, and their chattering inside her head to the unseen *Central* seemed like the clickings of insects. Like the insect, they labored with seemingly untiring energy; like the *krajal* they built their own colony home rather than take refuge in what nature afforded. And this Central, perhaps that was the queen, directing all activities of the hive.

The intricacy and sophistication of the city echoed in SilverSide. It awoke memories of her initial urges: *find sentient life. Find humans.* She'd made the decision on what was human, but the intelligence behind the Walking-Stones...

...but that was the province of the gods, or so LifeCrier's tales had indicated. A god had sent the WalkingStones as a god had sent SilverSide herself. It felt right to admire the genius that had created the WalkingStones, a resonance of the Third Law commands that had shaped her first hours. But admiration didn't mean that the WalkingStones weren't enemies. SilverSide had made her choice; the OldMother had sent her to the kin.

But still...The kin were human, yes, but SilverSide yearned for something more.

"Sometimes the *krajal* infest a place, too," LifeCrier was saying. "The queen breeds and breeds until the trees drip with the shiny bodies. They drop on the prey animals and bite, driving them mad until they flee. They can kill a youngling— a slow and horrible death."

LifeCrier closed his eyes, as if remembering. "The last time that happened, two LifeCriers ago, HalfTongue was the leader. During a storm, lightning struck a tree. HalfTongue noticed that the flames killed the *krajal* and that they fled. She took a branch from the tree and set a blue *krajali* on fire. The nearby reds came to defend it, leaving an opening. So Half-Tongue and the others took several burning brands and began using them to drive the *krajal* away until they could reach the queen and kill it. Once the queen was dead, the *krajal* behaved like crazy things and were easy to kill."

"WalkingStones won't burn. You can't burn a rock." KeenEye's comment was laced with her old scorn. If she was resigned to a secondary place in the pack behind SilverSide, she was also not going to submit to any of the other kin. "The WalkingStones would laugh at a burning stick."

SilverSide nodded in agreement, scenting KeenEye's irritation with LifeCrier's tales. "Still, there is a hint in LifeCrier's story. I must find out more about these WalkingStones. Keen-Eye, you will lead the pack in my absence. I will go down into the city. I need to discover if these other types of WalkingStones are more vulnerable than the Hunters. If what I suspect is true, then the Hunters will come after I attack. You must watch—see what they do, see how many they send and how quickly. Then go back to PackHome quickly. I will return by another route after I have made certain that no Hunters follow me."

"*If* you're not killed right away," KeenEye said. Her pale eyes were noncommital and SilverSide could not tell if the prospect pleased or disturbed her. "*If* you're right about these other WalkingStones."

"If anything happens to me, you become leader again," SilverSide answered. Yes, she scented satisfaction in KeenEye with that, and she continued. "But it won't. I don't intend to fight the Hunters. I only need to see how they react so we can plan. You can't hear them, but I can. The WalkingStones speak; they communicate as do the kin. I can use their language against them. I might be able to deceive them."

"GrayMane knew the language of the OldMother," Life-Crier said. "You see, KeenEye, it is as I said."

KeenEye grimaced, but she said nothing.

"Watch me for the time it would take to skin a deer," SilverSide told the group. "Remember what you see, every detail. It is very important. Then leave. Go directly back to PackHome." SilverSide used HuntTongue to accentuate the command.

KeenEye grimaced again, but she nodded. "As you wish."

SilverSide gave a soft bark of satisfaction. She looked at the pack, who watched the trio expectantly. The sight of the kin nudged a First Law circuit. "Keep them safe, KeenEye," SilverSide said. "Take them back as swiftly as they can go— the Hunters may come after you if I can't lead them away."

"I will do as SilverSide wishes," KeenEye answered in proud HuntTongue. "She does not have to worry."

There was nothing more to say. SilverSide glanced around the edge of the forest, making sure that no Hunters were lurking nearby. Swiftly, she dropped onto four legs and moved out into the wash of moonlight. She was a swift, glinting presence sliding into the shadows of the nearest buildings. SilverSide moved in among them several strides, then hunched down, belly to cool stone behind one of the structures.

She listened. The WalkingStones chattered to Central endlessly. Reports went in, orders went out. The WalkingStones were concentrated more toward the Hill of Stars where SilverSide suspected Central hid, but they occasionally moved through this area. She waited, patient.

When she heard the sound of a WalkingStone's tread, she allowed her body to deform slightly, extending an eyestalk around the corner of the building. The approaching WalkingStone was a spindly, gangly thing with arms tipped by mechanical claws rather than fingered hands. It was alone. SilverSide retracted the eyestalk, gathered herself; when the WalkingStone passed the side of the building, she leaped with a BeastTalk growl.

The WalkingStone's arms came up too late—SilverSide hit it, her jaws clamping around the thin, long neck and her powerful muscles shaking the thing from side to side. She was careful to hold her own great strength back and use no more power than any of the kin possessed.

That strength was enough, as she had suspected. These WalkingStones were far less durable than the Hunters. A support cracked; internal wiring harnesses tore. Just before the main trunk to the brain was severed and the WalkingStone went still under SilverSide's great bulk, she heard it call out to the distant Central.

Under attack. Damaged . . .

SilverSide let the thing slump to the ground. *Yes, as I thought.* The Hunters were designed to be the city's protection; the workers were strong but not overwhelming for a creature as powerful as the wolf-creatures. The worker WalkingStones, at least, were vulnerable.

And this also revealed another weakness. Not much of one, but it was all SilverSide had.

The voices in her head had gone silent. Replacing the chatter was an amplified voice, loud and commanding, resonating on all the frequencies. *Central. My enemy.*

And it did what she would have done herself. Central was sending the Hunters to investigate.

SilverSide didn't intend to be there when the Hunters arrived.

Giving a BeastTalk growl of triumph, she ran back toward the forest, staying where the kin could see her but not heading directly toward them. KeenEye would watch and make certain, then run to PackHome as ordered. SilverSide would make her way there herself, but first she had to make sure there was no latent danger to the kin.

It didn't matter if such a delay endangered her own self.

She waited until she caught a glimpse of the first Hunter moving swiftly along a walkway toward the area where the attack had occurred. *I am here,* she called to it in her own head voice, using the VoidTalk. The Hunter stopped, its armored head swiveling around.

SilverSide gave voice to a BeastTalk challenge and ran.

She was just about to duck under the cover of the trees when the laser hit her.

CHAPTER 12
A JOURNEY BEGINS

If this was the afterlife, it was damned uncomfortable.

For one thing, it was wet. He could feel water dripping on his face and body.

For another, being dead *hurt*.

Derec's ribs ached as if they'd been kicked repeatedly by an extraordinarily strong and stubborn mule. Most of his skin felt as if it had been scoured by a rough, rusty file, and what hadn't been scraped raw was parboiled. His head pounded with the great-granddaddy of all headaches, and he was afraid to open his eyes or try to sit up.

If this was eternity, it wasn't making a nice start.

But he couldn't lie there forever. Besides, there was a certain curiosity. . . .

There was definitely light beyond his eyelids. And beyond the dripping of water, he could hear a rushing, crackling noise like cellophane being crumpled.

Derec opened his eyes.

And, groaning, closed them again.

He was looking through a jagged hole in the ship's hull into a dull gray, rain-streaming sky. Through the curtain of rain, he could see a muddy hillside scored by some giant, maniac plow and sown with bright pieces of metal. Despite the storm, there was a fire smoldering in the grass a hundred meters away where one of the ship's drive engines lay half buried. A thick, greasy plume of black smoke was smeared across the sky under the racing clouds.

It didn't look good. Being alive was threatening to be more uncomfortable than being dead. "Mandelbrot?" Derec's voice was a hoarse croak. There was no answer.

"Mandelbrot?"

Still nothing. It looked as if he was going to have to get out by himself. He didn't like the idea, not one bit. Derec moved to unbuckle his crash webbing. It was a mistake.

He screamed and promptly blacked out again.

It had stopped raining and the grass fire was out when he came back to consciousness again.

"Reality, part two," he muttered to himself. There was still a throbbing ache in his left arm; his right seemed to be functioning, if badly bruised. He forced himself to look—yes, the left forearm was definitely fractured, the skin puffy and discolored, the arm canted at a slight and very wrong angle. The sight made him nauseous. *Great. All you need is to be sick all over yourself. What if you've got broken ribs or internal injuries. . . .*

Derec leaned his head back and took several deep breaths until his stomach settled again. Reaching over with his good hand, he tightened the left harness of the webbing until his shoulder was tight against the seat. Then he grasped his left arm at the wrist, took a deep breath, and held it.

And let it out again with a shout. He pulled, hard.

Bone grated against bone.

When Derec came to consciousness for the third time, he checked the arm. It was bruising nicely, but it looked straight now. He could wiggle his fingers, make a weak fist. The pain made him want to whimper, but there was nothing he could do about it for the moment.

"Okay," he breathed. "You got to get out, find the first aid kit, get the painkillers and the quick-knit pills," he told himself. "You can do it." Using his right hand, he unbuckled himself—squirming for the right-hand buckle at his shoulder, the pain stabbed at his chest: *broken ribs, too, if nothing worse*. He was starting to sweat, coldly, and the periphery of his vision was getting dark.

Shock. Take it easy. Just breathe for a few seconds.

Gingerly, Derec tried his legs. His left ankle had been wrenched badly, but he thought he might be able to put weight on it, and his right thigh was bloody under the torn pants, but everything worked.

Fine. Let's see if we can stand.

He pushed himself up with his one good arm, cradling the other. The movement coupled with the throbbing head made the ship swirl about him. For a moment, the world threatened to go away again. Derec fought to remain conscious. *No*, he pleaded. *The last thing you want to do is fall. You might not make it up again*.

After a minute, the landscape stopped its ponderous waltz around him, and he could stand. The cabin was a total loss. The flooring was buckled, gaping holes had been torn in the bulkheads, and everything was sitting at a slight downhill angle. Derec noticed Mandelbrot immediately. The pilot's seat had been sheared off during impact and lay on its side at the "bottom" of the cabin slope. Mandelbrot was still in the seat, his body dented, dinged, and scratched.

"Mandelbrot?" Derec called again, but there was still no answer. *First things first*, he told himself. *Where's that kit?*

It should have been on the near wall; it wasn't. After a stumbling search through the nearby rubble, Derec finally located the white-and-red box. He fumbled open the catch and tore open a vial of EndPain. He stabbed the injector into his thigh with a hiss of the air jet; the medication felt cool, and he could feel it spreading. The pain began to fade, the headache to ease. After a few minutes, he was feeling vaguely human again.

He found the quick-knit tabs, read the instructions, and swallowed two. With the pain temporarily subdued, he rigged a splint from a piece of plastic and the cloth covering of one of the seats. The arm felt better secured and placed in a sling. He knotted it with his teeth.

Derec was beginning to feel alive once more. Alive enough to know that he was still in deep trouble on a world he didn't know and maybe half a continent or more away from the Robot City and help. He could still hear the central computer via his chemfet link, but the damned thing still didn't respond to him as had the original—it would have been easy to order a squad of robots to find and rescue them.

And if pigs had wings . . .

Derec had to have Mandelbrot. Without the robot, this was going to be very, very touchy. The quick-knit tabs would heal his arm in a week or two—*if* he didn't refracture it rummaging through the wreckage; *if* there were no internal injuries that crippled him first; *if* there was nothing on this planet that decided he looked tasty. . .

If he was still *alive* in a week.

Derec made his slow way over the broken hull to the robot. The seat had pinned Mandelbrot to the wall. Derec braced his back against the cabin wall opposite the robot, planted his feet on the seat supports, and shoved: the seat groaned, moved, and dropped back again. Derec gritted his teeth, pushed once more. This time the seat tumbled over, Mandelbrot dangling loosely from the straps. Derec waited until his breath returned and then opened up the robot's chest cavity.

There were too many things that could have gone wrong with the robot that couldn't possibly be fixed here. Derec could imagine every last one of them in his mind.

It didn't look as bad as it might have. The trunk line from the main power source had pulled loose, though backup power to the brain was still intact: good, that meant there would be no memory loss. There was some structural damage, though Mandelbrot's Avery-type arm looked perfectly fine. The optical circuits had taken quite a jarring; Derec wouldn't be surprised if there were some problems there when he powered up the robot.

And it was going to be no fun working with one hand. "Only one way to find out . . ." he muttered, then shook his head. *Who in space are you talking to?*

It took an hour to find the toolbox; another to one-handedly splice the bad power cable and jury-rig the socket—he had to stop halfway through to hit the painkillers again; the headache was back and his ribs made every breath an agony. The soldering tip trembled in his hand as he made the last connections. He wiped sweat from his eyes and straightened. He closed the chest compartment and touched the power contact.

A status light blinked amber. One eye gleamed fitfully; the entire body shuddered. The head swiveled with a distressing squeal of grinding metal, and Mandelbrot looked in Derec's general direction.

"Master Derec?"

"Mandelbrot."

"You are very fuzzy in my optical circuits. It would appear that the landing was not all we had hoped for."

"It would appear so." Derec shrugged. "How are you?"

"Checking . . ." Mandelbrot's voice trailed off; the eye dimmed. After several seconds it brightened once more. "Systems check program running. Main positronic circuitry intact; two sectors damaged but recovered and backed up. Right optical circuits not functioning; left out of adjustment. Neck sleeve joint misaligned. Main trunk connections damaged but acceptable. Main and auxiliary power circuits acceptable. Three servo motors have cracked casings and will be a problem if the lubricant seals are breached and leaking. Knee servo in left leg burned out and knee locked." The robot's fingers clenched and opened. "Other minor damage. Would you prefer the full details?"

"Save it for later."

"Then I must ask how you are, Master Derec." Mandelbrot rose to his feet, the left leg extended stiffly. "I note that your arm is splinted and there is blood on your clothing. You grimace when you move, as if your chest hurts you."

"The arm's broken; it'll heal. I'm banged up but alive. I don't think it's anything serious. Considering the way we hit, we don't have anything to complain about."

"I was not complaining, Master Derec, simply trying to ascertain our status. Your health is of prime importance to me as you know. The First Law . . ."

Derec waved him silent. "We've done all we can do about that. Now we have to get ourselves out of here."

Gears whined drily as Mandelbrot surveyed the wreckage. "This was not a good landing," he said without inflection.

Derec laughed aloud despite the pain. After Robot City, he didn't know what to expect from robots: Mandelbrot had either acquired a certain irony and deadpan humor or come up with a good approximation of it. A First Law response to make him feel more comfortable or not, it worked. Derec grinned.

"Actually, it was probably your best." he said. "I'm surprised you got us down at all. What in the world happened?"

"I still am not sure, Master Derec. There was an alarm and then the impact. After that, I was too concerned with the ship to pursue the matter."

"I can believe it," Derec smiled. "Now let's see what we can salvage out of this mess."

It was a long, slow, and painful process. Most of the emergency food stores had been smashed or lost. Mandelbrot dredged up an inflatable survival tent and heater, rope, and a battery-powered lamp. On the down side, the communications gear was hopelessly ruined, as Derec found after an hour of trying to fit together pieces with the few spare parts on board.

The ship was a total loss. It would never see space again.

The salvaging efforts made a pitifully small pile outside the hull. At Derec's insistence, Mandelbrot split the burden in half; a pack for each of them. "You're hobbled, too," Derec pointed out in the face of Mandelbrot's insistence that the robot carry everything. "You'd be endangering me more by loading yourself up. I've got a bad arm; you've a bum leg and servos threatening to go at any time. You're half blind. Consider this a direct order and pick up your half."

Mandelbrot obeyed. "Good," Derec said. "Now—just where in the world are we going?"

"The Robot City was inland, Master Derec. I believe we are near the eastern coast. Since the sun is declining toward the hills, I would suggest that direction."

Derec gazed at the slopes to the west, green with a thick cover of trees. There'd be game under there, and plants to eat if the rations gave out. He sighed. There was little choice. They wouldn't make it off this planet until they had help, and the only help was Robot City. If the central computer wouldn't respond to his chemfet link, the robots would still give them any aid they requested, if only because the First Law required it.

We must look a sight, Derec thought as they walked away from the wreckage. *A lame robot and a beat-up man. At least the planet looks safe.*

CHAPTER 13

A CHASE THROUGH THE FOREST

The laser from the Hunter seared SilverSide's flank. She hadn't expected it to react so quickly.

With robotic speed, she leapt to one side and behind the cover of a thick tree trunk. The bark smoldered where her side pressed against it, and SilverSide modified her body to spread out thin fan-like structures to radiate away the excess heat. A spot of red gleamed on the tree by her head and SilverSide ducked once more—another Hunter, and this one coming from a different direction. She could see two more of the deadly WalkingStones hurrying along the walkways toward the edge of the city and the confrontation.

SilverSide howled and fled deeper into the woods. Along the ridge, she saw the rest of the pack, following her orders, turn back and flee toward PackHome. Now it was up to her— she had to get rid of the WalkingStones.

Ten minutes later, she was certain she'd lost them.

SilverSide had a decided advantage over the Walking-Stones in the forest. Her wolf shape was ideally suited for quick movement and lithe, accurate turns. Low to the ground, she could take advantage of brush and thickets for cover; knowing the forest as only a wolf-creature could, she was at ease finding the convoluted paths of the game animals. The WalkingStones seemed far less capable once they left the arrow-straight walkways and geometric patterns of their city.

SilverSide came to a halt in a glade a kilometer and a half from the valley of the WalkingStones. She halted, listening, scenting, and watching. Large moths flitted silently from tree to tree. A creature with huge suckers for feet hung upside down from a nearby branch. LargeFace spread silver lace patterns on the ground through the branches.

A branch cracked; a silver shape moved in the dark.

Central, the creature is here. The voice came from inside her head. *Ten degrees south, unit three. You should have a clear line of fire if you move forward.*

The darkness seemed to bother the WalkingStones as little as it did SilverSide, and it seemed that she had underestimated them. They were persistent and excellent trackers or they could not have followed her. They might be slower when moving in the trees, yes, but they seemed to be untiring.

And they had found her again.

Her logic circuits couldn't know disappointment or irritation or even fear, but the sight of the Hunters through the trees made her pause, made her growl softly in BeastTalk. They were not kin. These WalkingStones lacked all etiquette.

If they were human, she thought, *it would be easy. I could challenge their leader, and whomever won would lead all. That is the best way.*

But the WalkingStone's leader was Central, which was only a voice in her head, and the WalkingStones attacked kin like the SharpFangs, from hiding and without a proper challenge.

Like beasts. Like animals.

The Hunters were speaking with one another now, short bursts of high-pitched sound. SilverSide fingered the strands of semiconductors and colored wire around her neck. They were just made-things. Tools. They were *less* than animals, for all their sophistication. Yes, the technology made Silver-Side ache to know more, but they violated all her most primal urges.

She wanted desperately to break these tools.

A crisscrossing of sudden laser fire raked the underbrush. SilverSide pushed to her feet with a howl and ran again. She felt the awful heat of their weapons strike her, and she turned and twisted as she fled so that none of the beams could touch her for more than a few seconds. Even so, she could sense internal damage: automatic alarm circuits overloaded and caused emergency sub-routines to be run, rerouting her nerve signals along undamaged paths to the brain.

Again her wolf shape aided her as it had before; she outdistanced the Hunters quickly. But she could still hear them, could still smell that sharp tang of steel and lubricants. They would track her forever, she realized, and if they did that, they would find PackHome.

You cannot allow that to happen. The First Law was plain here.

A new positronic pathway opened, glimmering. Another robot might have kept running until it ran out of power or was caught. Another robot might have been trapped by inbuilt programming.

The Hunters were tracking a wolf, and though she had chosen that shape, it was not the only one she could be.

SilverSide's body began to alter. The great bulk of the wolf collapsed in on itself, the body becoming much smaller. The excess mass SilverSide squeezed outward, thinning it until the alloy was as thin as she could make it.

Great, powerful wings overshadowed her now. The wings beat, cupping air.

SilverSide flew.

She was a lousy bird. She was too massive, and there was nothing she could do to alter that. She didn't fly well, and she couldn't fly fast or high, but she flew.

Her moonshadow passed over the Hunters moving through the woods below.

The WalkingStones didn't even look up. A wolf that changed into a bird was not in their experience.

"You're certain you left them behind?"

The sun was just peeking over the edge of the hills, and most of the kin had come out to greet SilverSide as, in wolf form again, she loped from the forest. KeenEye prowled the packed ground outside the entrance to PackHome. She kept looking back into the fog drifting through the shafts of light under the trees.

"I am mostly certain," SilverSide replied. One of the pups came up to her and playfully nipped her back leg. She gently nudged the pup aside, and it ran back to its mother, yelping. "I was heading south away from the Hill of Stars, not toward here at all."

"They will follow your tracks and your scent." KeenEye would not let go of the argument, but at least it was in respectful KinSpeech and not HuntTongue, where SilverSide might have been compelled to challenge her.

"I became a bird. I left no tracks, and the wind took my scent."

"You became a bird. . . ." KeenEye's stance stiffened; she crouched slightly, offensively. That said more than her words.

"You doubt SilverSide, KeenEye?" LifeCrier asked mockingly. "You saw the Egg. You've seen her kill a Hunter, which none of us could do. You saw her kill another of the Walking-Stones and escape the Hunters' lightnings. We all know she's from the OldMother, and yet you scoff. *I* believe her, Keen-Eye, because I have listened to the tales of the OldMother. I have faith. What of the rest of you?"

The kin gave barks of agreement, and SilverSide could scent their pride in her. KeenEye's lips lifted, exposing teeth.

"It doesn't matter," she said disdainfully. "Bird or not, we've *still* done nothing about the WalkingStones. All we've accomplished is to anger them, and if they come *here,* to PackHome, we will all die. SilverSide might be able to kill one, but what of the rest of us?"

KeenEye's tail thrashed dirt. She fingered the necklace SilverSide had given her. "How many here have seen the bodies of kin slain by the Hunters?" she continued. "How many of you have pups who are thin because the meat is scarce? How many mothers have little milk to give the litters? We can't stand against the WalkingStones. And that is true with or without SilverSide, with or without the OldMother."

"Then we can go elsewhere," SilverSide suggested. "Give

the WalkingStones this place and find another."

"Where? We've already discussed that. The other packs already watch their borders, knowing the trouble we're having. No other pack will let us into their territory."

"Then you are telling me that we *must* stay here," Silver-Side said. "This is something I need to know—KeenEye, LifeCrier, all the rest of you. I do not know this world as you do. The OldMother left you the task of teaching me about the kin. *Must* we stay here?"

They nodded, howling softly. "In that, I'm afraid I must agree with KeenEye," LifeCrier said. "Our pack is already weak and small. In a fight with other pack-kin, we would all die."

That answer gave the logic circuits in SilverSide's brain the information they needed. Electrical synapses closed. It was simple.

The First Law demanded that human life must be protected. Her positronic brain, like every robot's, logically resolved inevitable conflicts to protect the many over the few. If the kin stayed here, the conflict would be human against WalkingStone. If they moved, another, uglier conflict must be confronted, and that would pit human against human. Silver-Side could not kill humans.

That realization allowed her to make an unpleasant decision. "Then we will stay here," she said, "and my choice is made for me."

"What choice?" KeenEye demanded.

"The choice to fight the WalkingStones."

"We *can't* fight them," KeenEye insisted.

"I know a way," SilverSide said. "I do not like it, but I know a way."

"Then speak. *Tell* us," KeenEye said, and the insolence was back in her voice, in her stance, in her smell. SilverSide stared at KeenEye, daring the former leader to challenge her again. SilverSide let her body enlarge slightly, her already massive chest puffing out. KeenEye growled and backed away.

"Kin will probably die, my way," SilverSide said, still looking at KeenEye. "But you tell me there is no other choice that is not worse. If you tell me wrong, you may well destroy the pack. If there *is* any way for us to go elsewhere, tell me now."

"There is no way," KeenEye said, snorting. She pawed at the ground with a clawed hand. "There are other packs all around us: OneEye's, ScarredPaw's. They've already said they will kill any of our litter-kin who trespass. Ask LifeCrier —he can tell you of the battles between packs. I didn't lie. And I'm not afraid to fight. Kin die all the time—it is part of the Hunt, it is part of defending territory."

"Then it is time to hunt WalkingStones," SilverSide answered.

"It is time to challenge them."

AROUND THE CAMPFIRE

It was difficult to hear anything above the racket Derec and Mandelbrot made moving through the woods. Derec quickly realized that there was no hope he'd be able to survive by hunting for food. He'd starve first.

They'd seen very little wildlife except during their rest periods. Otherwise, whatever animals lived here simply fled from the clamor of their passage. Shapes skittered through the trees ahead of them, birds took to the air with shrill cries. But a new sound intruded, making Derec cock his head quizzically.

"Did you hear that, Mandelbrot?"

Derec had stopped, leaning on the walking stick he'd cut from a dead branch and breathing heavily. They were struggling up a slope tangled with dense, close underbrush and tenacious, sticky-leaved vines; the place seemed to have been designed to give them trouble. The sun was already behind the hill and dropping rapidly, and Derec's legs itched wherever the plants had scraped skin through his clothing. Mandelbrot, ahead of him and sounding in dire need of an overhaul, was moving very slowly with his malfunctioning leg. The robot stopped and turned his head around, the neck grating metallically.

"I have heard several things, Master Derec. Which sound were you referring to?"

"The howling. There—you hear that?"

Very faintly, a mournful wail greeted the dusk. Another voice joined the first, then several others. The mournful chorus continued for several seconds, then went back to the solo voice once more. The forest seemed suddenly very dim and dangerous. Derec shivered involuntarily.

"That sends cold chills down my back," he said.

"There are thermal blankets in the pack," Mandelbrot told Derec. "Let me get one for you—"

Derec smiled. "It's not that kind of chill. It sounds like recordings I've heard of wolves—made before they became extinct."

The barking howls began again, echoing and reverberating among the slopes. Mandelbrot's neck joint screeched again as the robot looked upslope. "Their voices are complex," he said. "In some ways it reminds me of Wolruf's language."

Mention of the caninoid alien's name made Derec nod; he missed Wolruf, missed her quick wit and odd temper. "I wish it were, believe me. At least then we might get out of this mess. We have to find a place to camp for the night, Mandelbrot. Any level and halfway open space will do. I don't want to get caught out here in the open during the dark."

"My data banks say that even in the days before Earth was settled, most wild animals were afraid of humans. They very rarely attacked anyone without provocation."

"Well, I'm not going to count on them having been fed the same data. Let's keep going, Mandelbrot. Maybe at the top of this hill . . . though from the size of it I'm beginning to think we should promote it to mountain."

It took them another hour to struggle to the summit. There, the trees thinned out and finally disappeared on a wind-swept, rocky ledge that, looming above the surrounding hills, gave them an excellent vantage point.

Every last muscle in Derec's body ached from the exertion

of the climb. His broken arm throbbed and burned; he was breathing in quick gasps, afraid to breathe any deeper because of his ribs. Derec swung his pack down with a grimace and found the medical supplies. An EndPain injection allowed him to keep moving. Mandelbrot, every joint rasping, helped Derec inflate the tent and arrange their pitifully few supplies. Derec started a small fire in a circle of rocks, and they sat on the hilltop watching the stars appear in the dark blue of the zenith, sprinkled across the sky in their millions.

"They certainly are persistent, those wolves or whatever they are." The howls had continued to serenade them as they'd made camp. They seemed to be coming from the west, in the same general direction they were heading though several hills over. Derec sat on the edge of the ledge and tossed pebbles into the trees below, listening to them crash through the branches. He looked at the shadowy landscape ahead of them and grimaced. "Look at that. You'd figure the hills would all have to run north and south—we're going to walk five kilometers up and down for every one due west."

Derec glanced over at the robot standing alongside him. It didn't seem to have heard. "Mandelbrot?"

"I am sorry, Master Derec. I was listening to them."

"Just make sure they don't get closer." Derec threw another stone, then squinted toward the west. "How well are you seeing, Mandelbrot?"

"My night vision is very poor due to the crash damage. It is no better than yours."

"Uh-huh. Take a look anyway and tell me if that isn't a glow in the northwest, maybe four or five of those hills over. I didn't notice it before, but with the darkness—"

Mandelbrot peered in the direction Derec was pointing. "I see a patch of light reflecting from underneath clouds. . . ."

Then, for a moment, they were both silent, listening to a voice that whispered in both their heads.

All units: central computer under attack. All units . . .

The voice was very faint. It faded even as Derec tried to get the voice to respond.

"My fa—" Derec began, then stopped himself. He hated the man too much to call him that, and on Aurora it meant very little anyway. "Mandelbrot, it must be Avery."

"It is possible."

"It's more than possible. It explains everything: the distress call, the central computer not responding to the chemfets, our crash-landing—everything. He could have used a Key, jumped to the Compass Tower here, and started disrupting the city."

"Why?" Mandelbrot asked. "The first Robot City was his creation."

"He was also very disturbed that I could control it. Maybe he's decided to destroy all the others."

"It is possible, I suppose," Mandelbrot admitted. "But we will not know until we arrive."

"We have to push harder, Mandelbrot. The city's in trouble."

"Why should that concern you so much, Master Derec?"

The question sounded like one Ariel might have asked, and the reminder hurt more than his physical pain. Derec scowled. "It just does. Maybe it's the chemfets—some chemical bonding with the city that's due to them. I don't *know*, Mandelbrot. All I can tell you is that I hurt when the city hurts, and it makes me want to do something about it. Can you understand that?"

"I can, Master Derec. What you describe sounds very similar to the compulsion of the Three Laws within every robot. And if we must push ourselves tomorrow, I would suggest that you rest," the robot said gently. "You are exhausted, and I cannot carry you."

Derec wanted to argue, but Mandelbrot was right. He could feel the weariness; and the effort it took to get to his feet convinced him. "Then I'm going to try to sleep. What about you?"

"I do not know how much longer I will be able to walk. The less I move, the better. I will stand here and watch. Have a good sleep."

His dreams were haunted by his father, who could take on the shape of a wolf. Ariel was there, but wolf-Avery chased her away, and though Derec tried to run after her, his feet were leaden and horribly slow.

Derec awoke with a start. For a moment, he was disoriented and nearly panicked until the nagging pain in his arm and ribs reminded him. He opened the tent and poked his head out through the flaps.

It was still dark. Two moons were in the sky; one high, the larger one low to the west. Backlight against the moonlight, he could see Mandelbrot, standing motionless at the edge of the overlook and staring out into the night. He could hear the wolf-creatures baying at the moon.

"Mandelbrot?"

"Everything is fine, Master Derec. I was listening to them. Their voices; it is almost like a language."

"Their voices make me want to avoid them at all costs. They're probably discussing how tasty my bones and your metal would be. Good night, Mandelbrot."

"Good night, Master Derec."

He lay there for a long time in the darkness, not wanting to go to sleep. He didn't know if it was because Avery would be waiting for him in his dreams, or because he was afraid Ariel would not.

CHAPTER 15

FEINT AND THRUST

SilverSide's creator herself might have been distressed by the robot's logic. Janet Anastasi might well have been appalled and considered SilverSide's positronic mind to be hopelessly damaged. It is impossible to say.

Surely an Auroran robot would have been crippled, if not driven into outright positronic lockup, by the implications of this decision. But to SilverSide, the Three Laws were simply the morals of the OldMother, and her logic and her interpretations were not shaped by human standards, but by those of the kin.

Inclined to respond physically and aggressively to a challenge.

It took the pack another day to prepare, a long day of using their "found" tools such as sticks and flat stones, their few flint-shaped blades and planes. No one was exempt; even the very old and the very young helped as far as they were able.

After SilverSide was satisfied with the arrangements, she sent most of the kin back to PackHome after warning them to take a circuitous, long route. She sent some of the hunting kin with them for protection, not wanting to leave PackHome entirely undefended should her plan fail. KeenEye and LifeCrier insisted on remaining behind with SilverSide, and she chose another half-dozen of the pack to stay as well.

As the sun set, they said their farewells to the rest of the kin and watched them make their way among the trees. When they were gone, SilverSide howled a long challenge to the rising moons and turned to the others.

"Now, let us go find a WalkingStone to kill," she said.

The city had changed, even in the two days since she had last seen it. It had encroached farther on the forest, spilling from the valley that had confined it. Worker WalkingStones with roaring chainsaws for arms were tearing at the trees at the leading edge of the city; farther in toward the Hill of Stars, everything seemed to have changed. The ice-blue building to the west had been farther over and shorter the last time, and the flying buttresses linking it to the building alongside had not been there at all. The cluster of geodesic domes at the base of the Hill of Stars was certainly new, and an open space lush with greenery yawned under the bright lights of a slender needle tower. It was as if the WalkingStones were not satisfied with their expansion; they had to tear down and rebuild even in the center of their city.

The valley was awash in them. The wind stunk of metal; the VoidEyes in the sky above were lost in the glare.

Yet the WalkingStones' ceaseless toil impressed SilverSide, even as she growled at the sight of the naked, muddy hillsides in their path.

"They rape the land, like a male taking a female before her time," KeenEye snarled. She growled in BeastTongue: a sound of pure loathing. "There are always more of them, always more of their stone caves, always more of their lights and noise and smells."

"They leave nothing for us," LifeCrier agreed. "Is this the way the Void looks, SilverSide? Is this the way the gods live?"

"I do not know," SilverSide answered. "It is possible. I feel . . . I feel a pull to it, LifeCrier. There is something in the smoothness, in the many tools they use, in the way they move. Perhaps it is something I once knew."

"Then the gods can have the Void," KeenEye said in irreverent KinSpeech. "I hate it."

"OldMother will eat the souls of kin as we rise to the Void," LifeCrier chastised the former leader, using HuntTongue to emphasize his point. "She takes us to the One Pack again, and we run in the Endless Forest."

SilverSide snapped at the two of them. "Silence!" she ordered. LifeCrier immediately moved back into the pack; KeenEye stared at SilverSide for a moment, then dropped her muzzle. "Move forward now. Quietly. We don't want to bring the Hunters too quickly."

The pack flowed among the trees following SilverSide. She brought them to a halt near the cleared section downwind of the WalkingStones and surveyed the area.

"There," SilverSide whispered, pointing. "They will do."

The wall of a building rose several meters away, a building under construction. A group of three WalkingStones was hauling materials to a wheeled cart alongside the wall, their backs to the forest. The workers were isolated, most of the continuing work being done in a floodlit area half a kilometer away. Their head-voices were silent.

"Now," SilverSide said, and leaped into the open.

As one, the pack followed her, sweeping across the ground like a gray wind and then falling on the WalkingStones with savage growls. SilverSide took one of them by the throat, shaking with all her robotic strength and feeling the hated thing die before it could sound an alarm. The others hit the remaining two WalkingStones in a rush.

Central! Under attack—

SilverSide heard the distress call cut off in mid-sentence even as she turned to help KeenEye and the others. She needn't have been concerned. As she had suspected from her encounter with the other worker, the kin's strength was great enough to disable this species of WalkingStone. Under the floodlights across the open field, other workers were looking at them, and SilverSide heard them alerting Central to the pack's presence.

She grasped KeenEye's shoulder. "The Hunters will be coming. We must go."

"Then we'll meet them here," KeenEye said. Her eyes were bright with the death of the WalkingStones.

"No," SilverSide said in emphatic HuntTongue. "KeenEye will destroy the pack if she does that. We've prepared for them—they will follow. I promise that. Take them; I'll follow."

KeenEye gave a howl of both challenge and triumph to the nearest workers and turned. The pack followed her back into the forest. SilverSide waited, standing over the downed workers. Yes, they were like the *krajal*. The others had turned back to their work, following the orders of Central. She heard Central call the Hunters. When she saw the first gleam of their armored skin rushing toward her, she turned and followed the path of the others back into the forest.

Behind her, she heard the crashing as the Hunters bulled their way into the undergrowth.

SilverSide snaked her way through the trees, making sure she stayed well ahead of them but left a clear path behind. Even so, the WalkingStones remained close behind her. When she finally broke through into the glade where the others waited, they were not far behind. All the kin could hear them; birds were rising in panic above the trees, and they could smell the oily stench. The kin stirred restlessly, muttering in angry BeastTalk as they milled around SilverSide.

She stood in the center of the glade, pacing. The open spot was situated in a deep valley, surrounded on all sides but one by steep slopes. "The rest of you—into the trees and make ready," she ordered. "Do not let them see you. Remember that their lightning will kill you if it touches you. I will lure them in and then run. KeenEye, you will do the rest."

They were barely in position when the first of the Hunters broke through the ring of trees, the others at its heels. Silver-Side gave a rumbling BeastTalk challenge, then broke and ran when the Hunters raised their hands to her. Laser fire raked the trees, just missing her, and the Hunters lumbered into motion again. *Follow*, the voices in her head said. *Do not let the creature escape this time*.

This was exactly what SilverSide had hoped for. The hillsides formed a natural funnel; the WalkingStones had to move as a group. The WalkingStones moved across the glade as one.

And, as one and intent on their pursuit of SilverSide, they tumbled into the deep pit the kin had dug across the glade and hidden with dry grass.

"Now, KeenEye!" SilverSide cried.

The dirt removed from the pit had been piled next to it and blocked with fallen logs. Now KeenEye cut the lashings holding the logs. They rolled crazily over the edge, followed by a roaring landslide of dirt and stones. The kin pushed at the mounds of dirt, howling, keeping it cascading down on the Hunters as a choking cloud of dust rose. SilverSide could hear the head-voices wailing distress as the WalkingStones were covered under the weight of two meters of rocky clay.

When the dust settled at last, there was nothing to be seen of the Hunters. They were gone. Buried. Even the head-voices were silent.

The pack howled and wailed in BeastTalk. They clambered over the pit, stomping on the earth that hid the WalkingStones and packing it down. LifeCrier licked SilverSide's cold muzzle; even KeenEye rubbed her flank in appreciation. "We've done it!" LifeCrier sighed. "We've killed Hunters. All the kin can see the gift of the OldMother now."

The reminder served to temper KeenEye's satisfaction. The former leader only grunted. "It might seem so. But this was only one battle, LifeCrier. Only half of SilverSide's plan. There's still the rest."

SilverSide nodded in agreement and the mood of the kin darkened again. The celebration ended as they gathered around her again. "All of you must stay here to watch," she told them when they were quiet. "Central may send workers to dig these Hunters out, or it may have other Hunters to send. KeenEye, your task is harder than mine. You must watch. If other Hunters come, flee, but remember that you cannot go back to PackHome until you have lost them. No matter what, you must keep them occupied for as long as you can. If workers come, you must stop them from unearthing these Hunters, or if you find that the Hunters can dig themselves out somehow, you must find a way to stop them or slow them down. We've not won. Not yet. We've only made the first step."

SilverSide picked up a clod of dirt and crumpled it in her hand, letting the dust trickle back through her long, clawed fingers. "Now, I must go and find this Central."

"They have been following us for the last few hours, Master Derec."

"I know. I can hear them."

Derec didn't like the sound of the long, quavering howls echoing among the hills. He also didn't like the fact that the sun was just ready to set.

Their last few days had been slow and painful, but mostly uneventful. Mandelbrot's knee had seized up entirely; the robot walked with a stiff-legged limp that made their progress halting. Derec's arm was still sore and throbbing, but he nursed the remaining painkillers, taking them only when it became unbearable. He watched his own footing carefully, knowing that if he stumbled he couldn't easily break his fall. Derec would have sworn that their backpacks, light enough when they'd started out, seemed to be gaining weight as the days wore on.

He wasn't much enjoying his first days on this world. He would have given nearly anything for a hovercraft. His feet hurt, his boots rubbed his toes raw, he'd found a hundred bruises he hadn't known he'd had, and they had no idea if they'd ever see the Robot City that still adamantly refused to talk to him.

What good are the chemfets if you can't communicate both ways?

It was just like something Dr. Avery would do. More and more he was convinced that he would find Avery here, that Avery would somehow be behind it all.

Worst of all, he missed Ariel. He missed her terribly. He'd replayed their argument over in his head a thousand times. He'd come up with a hundred lines that would have made it better, if only he had a chance to do it over again. It would have been so easy.

Okay, Ariel. I'm sorry. Come with us. Please.

But of course there was no way to go back in time and tell her that. There was no way for him to turn back the clock and stop the argument before it began. It would always be there between them. The best he could hope for was that she'd be willing to forgive him when he returned to Aurora.

If he returned to Aurora.

All in all, Derec sorely regretted his decision to come to this place.

And now there were wolves.

They had been shadowing Derec and Mandelbrot since yesterday, always staying out of close range but always just on the edge of sight.

"I believe it is a territorial problem," Mandelbrot said. "I think we are just on the edge of their land and they are warning us away."

"We're not going to harm them. We just want to get to Robot City."

"That doesn't seem to be something they would understand, Master Derec."

Derec stopped and slipped the pack from his back, grimacing as the straps put weight on his broken arm. There was a compressed-air gun in the survival gear, a short-range weapon only, but the glass darts contained a deadly nerve poison. Derec felt Mandelbrot watching him as he loaded the gun and slid the holster on his belt. "They could be carnivores," he said to the robot. "I don't want to take any chances."

"I have been listening to them," Mandelbrot said. "The calls are remarkably complex."

"And their teeth may well be remarkably sharp."

"Understood, Master Derec. Still, I have been carefully watching and listening. They seem to be staying within these hills." Mandelbrot pointed to the area directly ahead of them. "One of them will come directly into view and howl to us, like a challenge or warning—that is why I believe they are telling us to turn away. What if their calls are a language? Perhaps we should avoid confrontation all together."

"How? By going a hundred kilometers around? Mandelbrot, we're both hurt. We need help, and the only help is in Robot City. Which is—we think—that way. Wolves or no wolves. I've heard the wolves, too, and it doesn't sound like any kind of language to me."

"I understand, Master Derec. Still, the voices *are* very complex: the falling tones, the breaks . . ."

"We don't have time for detours. We won't live long enough for that."

Mandelbrot nodded. Derec's insistence forced First Law overtones and Third Law obedience: the robot went silent. They began walking again.

Long shadows covered the landscape; the disc of the sun was gone behind the hills, and the western sky was a bath of crimson. Already the first stars were up in the east, with the largest of the two moons a crescent horn high in the sky.

Derec and Mandelbrot used the remaining light to push on into the hills. The barks and yips and howls stopped ominously as they topped the first crest. When it became too dark to see the tree roots and stones in their path, they stopped. Derec unpacked the tent; Mandelbrot made a fire. "Wolves are often afraid of fire," Mandelbrot said.

"I'll remember to hire you as a guide next time we go on safari," Derec said. Firelight threw moving, wavering shadows through the trees; the wood hissed and sparked, and it was hard to see anything beyond the glare of the flames. Derec thought it worse than the darkness itself. It was easy to imagine shapes in the erratic light, and none of the shapes in Derec's mind was pleasant.

"I'll get some food started—" Derec began to say.

And then the shapes from his nightmares streaked from the woods, growling and snarling.

They were not wolves, at least not like any wolves Derec knew. They were larger than the old pictures Derec had seen: lean, gray-furred bodies and massive chests, their heads peculiarly shaped, large-skulled but with a distinct canine muzzle. They ran from the woods on all fours but reared up on the hind legs at will, slashing with forepaws—well-articulated fingers tipped with razor claws. Their eyes were red from reflected firelight, and they roared and howled and shrieked as they attacked.

The creatures hit Mandelbrot first, which very likely saved Derec's life. They ignored Derec, slamming into the hobbled robot. Mandelbrot could not move quickly enough to avoid them. The robot flailed back at them, the Avery arm snaking like a whip. It struck one of the wolves across the snout and there was a distinct crack of bone as the wolf-creature yelped, rolled, and fled.

Three more struck Mandelbrot at once, and the impact, combined with Mandelbrot's bad leg, knocked the robot entirely over. He fell into the fire, clasping two of the attacking wolf-creatures. Sparks flared and snapped; the wolves howled in fear and pain as they struggled to get away from the robot's steel grasp. Mandelbrot let them go at last and the wolves yelped and fled, their fur scorched and burning. Mandelbrot struggled to get back on his feet, sending glowing embers flying through the air.

Then everything was confused. Derec had dragged the gun from its holster. He squeezed the trigger at anything moving beyond the campfire; the gun bucked in his hand. Something big and horribly strong hit him from behind and he went down, shouting with pain and nearly losing consciousness as he landed on his bad arm. He couldn't see anything; his head was full of exploding blotches. Somehow Derec held onto the gun and fired blindly. He couldn't tell if he hit anything or not, but all at once the battle was over. One of the wolves gave a short, high bark; the others dropped the attack and fled into the woods.

Derec felt a metallic hand on his shoulder. "Master Derec?"

"Wolves are afraid of fire, huh?"

"I have made the correction in my data bank."

"Good. Wonderful. Now help me up."

The camp was a mess. Burning logs were scattered around the area; the tent had collapsed. There was a long rip in one of the packs, and several cans of food had spilled out. "Great," Derec sighed. "We'll be up half the night fixing things. *If* our friends don't make a return visit," he added. "Man's best friend, they aren't."

They found the body in the morning as they began their trek once more. Derec nearly stumbled over it in the under-brush. "What the—" he began, then stopped.

"Oh, no," Derec said breathlessly. "Please, no."

"What is it, Master Derec?" Mandelbrot said, limping over.

Derec didn't answer. He only stared.

The wolf-creature had evidently caught one of the stray darts Derec had fired the night before. It was a young one, a female who had evidently been watching the fight from the cover of the trees. She certainly had not been involved herself.

She couldn't have, even if she'd wanted to. Lashed around her body with vines was a primitive *travois* built of trimmed sticks, a carrier. And in one hand, uselessly, she clenched a stone knife the chipped edges of which showed the mastery of a flint knapper.

"By any god you care to name . . ." Derec breathed. "Man-delbrot, you were right. The wolves—they're *sentient*."

Derec looked at the body, stricken. "And I killed one."

CHAPTER 17

IN THE HILL OF STARS

She bayed a challenge to Central from the nearest hill, for no kin would go into battle with an equal without first warning them.

There was no answer. She hadn't expected one.

Packing along the hills at the edge of the city, SilverSide watched for several minutes, paying careful attention to the movements of the nearest WalkingStones and listening to their voices in her head.

There were several types that seemed to roam freely through the streets. SilverSide left the heights and moved down from the trees to get a closer look at them. She ran quickly across the cleared area around the spreading city and into the shadows of the buildings. When one of the Walking-Stones passed her hiding place, SilverSide quickly memorized its shape and walk; once it was gone, SilverSide willed her body to change once more, patterning herself after the Walk-ingStone. Her head became round and smooth; her body straightened and she stood upright, letting the markings of the kin disappear.

When it was done, she took the necklace of wires from her head and laid the token of her first victory on a ledge. She walked onto the hard stone walkways and eternal daylight of the city.

SilverSide watched and listened carefully for any sign of recognition or alarm in the first few WalkingStones she passed, but none of them paid her any attention at all. As she went deeper into the steel canyons of this place, the Walking-Stones became more numerous. Soon SilverSide was moving in great crowds of them, of all manner of shapes and sizes. This was certainly not the forest, where a kin could—at need —wander for a day or more without seeing another of the kin. LifeCrier's analogy, which had first sparked this idea in her, seemed more and more apt. These were *krajal*, hive-insects. They could not exist without each other. They had no individuality at all. They existed only to serve Central, and without Central they were nothing.

Their society seemed very wrong to SilverSide. Her decision now gave her no pause at all. It was right to destroy this place, despite the sophisticated technology it showed. It spoke of intelligence, yes, but of intelligence used in the wrong way. This was not logical, she decided. This was not the way of humans.

SilverSide continued on. The kin, she knew, would have been puzzled by the silence of the city: there were few noises at all beyond the hum of machinery and the sound of the WalkingStones' passage. None of them spoke in what the kin would have considered an audible range. But SilverSide heard the racket of their thousands. She listened to the Walking-Stones' endless chatter in her head. Already she was missing the good smell of earth and foliage and the sounds of life. This was a dead place. This was a sterile and horrible place, and she was headed for the very heart of it.

The Hill of Stars. There, Central would be waiting for her. LifeCrier had said that the Hill of Stars was the first thing the WalkingStones had built. The *krajal* always built first a room for their queen.

The different species of WalkingStones all used different frequencies to communicate with Central—SilverSide knew that without understanding frequencies or bandwidths: each species resonated in a slightly different place in her head.

Janet Anastasi had also built into her robot a primitive location device: SilverSide could listen to Central and know from which direction the transmission came.

It was easy enough to walk the streets and listen, tracking Central. None of the workers even questioned her right to be there; they ignored her, going about their own tasks.

Central was concerned about her, though. SilverSide heard a continuous stream of unanswered queries directed to the Hunters. As she approached the Hill of Stars itself, Central ordered a group of workers into the forest to seek the Hunters. SilverSide felt satisfaction at that, for it meant that Central either had no more Hunters to send or that it was not going to expend more of them until it understood what had happened. Either way, it meant that the other kin were relatively safe for the moment.

SilverSide continued on until she reached the large open plaza in which the Hill of Stars stood.

The gigantic pyramidal structure overshadowed any of the other buildings in the city, towering higher than the hills surrounding the valley. Its steep, sloping faces were pocked with windows behind which she could occasionally see one the WalkingStones moving. The scale of the structure was something she could only now begin to understand. It was immense, far larger than anything else in this place. A fitting place for the Central, for this queen WalkingStone, she decided. There were large doors cut into each of the sides. SilverSide began walking across the plaza toward the nearest of them.

She expected to be stopped and challenged. She had prepared herself to be ready to move quickly and violently, knowing that once an alarm was raised, Central would immediately take steps to protect itself, and she would have scant minutes to finish her task.

It was almost too easy. None of the WalkingStones in the plaza made any move to prevent her from entering the Hill of Stars. Like the rest, they paid no attention to her at all. She was simply another one of the workers, going silently about her task without question—why should another of them question her right to be there? She entered into a cold dimness bounded by stone and cut with wide hallways.

There were fewer of the WalkingStones here, and most of them had a different body construction: more streamlined, with hands obviously designed for delicate work. From the orders given them by Central, SilverSide knew that these were the attendants of Central, the ones allowed into its presence. SilverSide let her body change to match their shape in a brief moment when she was alone in the hall and then continued walking, waiting.

It took only a few minutes. An order came from Central to one of the attendants who had just passed SilverSide, summoning it. The WalkingStone turned to obey, and SilverSide followed, moving with the WalkingStone along the labyrinthian corridors deeper into the heart of the Hill of Stars. In time, they passed through a set of wide doorways into a vast interior chamber.

And SilverSide looked upon Central.

The huge chamber was brightly lit from hanging lamps. Four doors entered into it on the ground level; balconies rimmed the walls to the ceiling, twenty or more stories high. In all that vast space, WalkingStones moved on all sides, but the ground floor was left mostly empty but for a cluster in the exact middle. There stood a quartet of Hunters, one at each corner of an array of eight wafer-thin, two-meter-tall rectangles, arranged like the rays of a stylized sun around a central column. The column was all black and chrome, with tiny lights blinking red and amber up and down its length. The presence of the Hunters would have been enough, but Silver-Side could sense the power and energy coming from the structures.

Central. The Queen. The mind behind the WalkingStones.

And with the Hunters guarding it, SilverSide knew that a frontal attack would not work. She altered her course in what she hoped looked to be a purposeful way, angling toward another of the exits from the room. One of the Hunters watched her, but she heard nothing in her head from Central. Silver-Side left the room and went into the hallway beyond.

Had she been kin, she might have felt despair. Isolated as it was, with the Hunters around it, there seemed to be no way to reach Central. It would be a long run across that floor; before she could hope to reach the unit, she would be cut down by the Hunters' laser fire. As for the balconies . . .

She passed a glassed-in elevator rising toward the top of the Hill of Stars, climbing the outside of Central's chamber. The glimmer of an idea sparked in her positronic brain.

SilverSide stepped into the open door of one of the elevators as another of the WalkingStones stepped off. A row of marked buttons was set next to the door; she pressed one and the elevator rose swiftly up, stopping gently with a chime. SilverSide stepped out and found the nearest door leading into the central chamber. She stepped to the railing and looked down.

Far, far below in that dizzying space, she could see the sunray design of Central.

Any Third Law requirement that she protect her own life was lost in the First Law possibilities represented by the death of Central. The fact that she might die in the effort meant nothing weighed against the fact that it would save the lives of kin. SilverSide climbed up on the railing, her body changing back to wolf shape. Her powerful hind legs gathered.

She leapt.

Her robotic strength took her out over the well of emptiness. At the zenith of her leap, over the center of the space, she willed herself to change once more, letting the body expand and thin and flatten into a glider shape like the paraseeds she'd seen fall from the trees near PackHome. She sailed, soaring and spiraling down—a silent enemy descending.

For several seconds, she heard nothing. SilverSide began to think that this would work, that she would plummet unhindered down to Central.

But a worker pointed as she passed one of the balconies in her descent. SilverSide realized that there were certain things too out of the ordinary for even the workers to ignore.

Central! Alert!

The Hunters looked up and saw SilverSide.

• • •

One of the younglings heard them first. "KeenEye," he hissed. "WalkingStones!"

KeenEye growled in BeastTalk. Since SilverSide had left, she had been prowling the ground where the Hunters were buried, nervous and agitated. She'd been expecting this. She'd known that this was a foolhardy idea from the beginning. But SilverSide was the leader—there was nothing she could do about that short of challenging her again, and Silver-Side was simply too strong. KeenEye gave LifeCrier a baleful, accusing glance and bounded toward the youngling.

"Go see where they are," she ordered the young male. "Quickly!"

"SilverSide hasn't had time yet to destroy Central," Life-Crier said, coming up behind KeenEye as she watched the youngling rush away. "Only a few more minutes—"

"Or perhaps she's already been killed and this is a squad of Hunters who will kill the rest of us."

"SilverSide is the OldMother's—"

"Be quiet!" KeenEye growled in savage HuntTongue. "I am tired of hearing this prattling about OldMother and the Void. SilverSide has made a mistake, whether she is from the OldMother or not."

"And what would you have done, KeenEye? Would you let us slowly starve to death? At least SilverSide is trying to do something about the WalkingStones."

Their argument went no further. The youngling came back panting. "They are workers," he gasped, his head lolling and his tongue out. "But one of them has hands like the Hunters. That one walks in front, like a leader."

"SilverSide had said that Central might send workers," LifeCrier said.

"She didn't say that they would have the weapons of the Hunters, though, did she?" KeenEye glowered. "If they're workers, then we will destroy them as we did the others. They will be expecting us here. LifeCrier, you will go to the west and circle to come behind them; I will go east and do the same. The rest of you will hide in the trees until these workers begin to dig. Then we'll hit them from all sides at once. Make sure the first one attacked is the one with Hunter's hands."

KeenEye looked at each of the small group of kin and lapsed back into KinSpeech, gruffly affectionate. "We must stop them from unearthing the Hunters. We must try to give SilverSide the time she asked for." She looked at LifeCrier last of all. "Even if it means nothing," she added. "Now— go!"

KeenEye and LifeCrier streaked away as the others melted into the cover of trees around the glade.

CHAPTER 18
ENCOUNTER WITH KIN

The wolf-creatures did not attack again that day, though Derec and Mandelbrot heard them often or glimpsed them shadowing their progress through the trees. Derec watched them, his weapon at ready but not certain that he could fire it again, not with the knowledge that they were intelligent. Once or twice, he called out to the wolves or gestured to one of them slipping past, but they never responded.

By noon, the calls had faded behind them, and they were left alone in the forest.

"I think we must have passed only through a far corner of their territory," Mandelbrot said. "The attack was simply to ensure that we came no closer to their den or whatever, and they stayed with us to be certain that we left. It is a lucky accident that our path did not lead us in the wrong direction."

"It would have been luckier if it hadn't led us to them at all," Derec answered morosely.

"We must be very careful," Mandelbrot said. "There are likely to be more tribes in the area. Master Derec, do you think that perhaps these wolf-creatures would be able to help us? Perhaps we do not have to find the Robot City."

"No," Derec replied, but the question made him glance

97

over to Mandelbrot. "We need Robot City. Stone Age technology won't do either of us any good. Are you going to repair your knee with a flint joint? Are you going to find servos and high-grade lubricants and a new optical circuit?"

Mandelbrot was silent after that, but Derec knew that the robot was experiencing a mental quandary after their encounter with the wolf-creatures. Mandelbrot was obviously troubled by their sentience. It showed in the questions he asked, in the way that he looked at Derec's weapon, in the attention the robot paid to the movement of the wolf-creatures watching them.

Knowing the robot as he did and having seen the reactions of the original Robot City robots to Wolruf, Derec knew where the problem lay. He could almost hear balances shifting within the robot's mind.

"Mandelbrot," he said as they walked, "how do you regard the wolf-creatures? How do the Laws apply to them?"

"Are you asking if I consider them 'human,' Master Derec?"

"Yes. I suppose that's the basic question. Are they human? I know you came to class Wolruf as human."

"Positronic minds are as variable as those of humans, Master Derec. What *is* human? There are many ways to answer the question, all of them valid and all of them with shortcomings. Certainly it is more than simply the way a being looks; even among the humans I have seen there is a great variance."

Derec was shaking his head. "But every one of them you've encountered has been Homo sapiens, a bipedal, upright-walking mammal descended from apes and able to trace their ancestry back to Earth. These wolf-things, whatever they are, aren't bipedal, aren't apes, and aren't descended from anything on Earth."

"That description fits Wolruf as well."

"Point taken. But you haven't answered my question yet. Let me give you a hypothetical situation: If I told old Balzac back on Aurora that Wolruf was a great danger to me and the only way to remove the danger was to kill her, would Balzac do it?"

"The danger would have to be demonstrated, Master Derec. Your word would not be enough."

"All right, assume it was. Assume I can convince Balzac of the imminent risk. I know I couldn't order Balzac to kill a human, but what about Wolruf? Balzac's seen her walk and talk and use the computer and pilot a ship. Would he still be able to protect me?"

Mandelbrot's eyes gleamed. His bad leg dragged through underbrush, and the robot came to a halt alongside Derec. "You are asking this because you are concerned that I will not be able to protect you should these wolf-creatures attack again."

Derec shrugged. He patted his broken arm, then waggled the gun in his hand. "We're not in the greatest of shapes, Mandelbrot. Neither one of us. First, I don't want to have to use this thing, not after what we know now, but if I have to in order to stay alive, I probably will. What about you, Mandelbrot?"

The robot seemed to consider that for a long moment, and for a moment Derec was afraid that he might have inadvertently driven the robot into positronic lockup. Then servo motors whirred as it began walking again. "I have searched my data banks and checked the functions of my logic system, Master Derec, and the readouts are very erratic. My priority circuits are almost in balance. Had I never met Wolruf, had I never seen sentient alien lifeforms, and did I not have memories of Robot City in my mind, I am sure it would be different."

"What are you saying, Mandelbrot?"

"That I do not know what I would do, Master Derec. I do not know."

He could have insisted. He could have made it a direct question and stressed the importance of an answer—the Second Law would have forced Mandelbrot to answer. *"Mandelbrot, do you consider these wolf-creatures to be as human as me?"*

But somehow it didn't seem right to ask.

After all, Derec wasn't sure of the answer himself.

All of the sudden, it was too late to ask.

They had continued to walk even after the sun had set. The moons were up and bright, and Derec wanted to cover as much ground as they could before settling for the night.

Mandelbrot's comlink overheard the short-range call. "Derec," it said. "There are robots in the near vicinity." Mandelbrot's flat, emotionless voice sounded strangely dispassionate. "They seem to be searching for Hunter-Seekers that are also supposed to be in this vicinity."

Derec couldn't help the grin that split his face. "That's wonderful, Mandelbrot. Now we can finally get out of here." He focused his thoughts inward, trying to contact the robots via the chemfets in his body, but the link was still not there. "Can you contact them, Mandelbrot? Tell them there's a human in need of aid—"

Derec got no farther.

A fury in gray fur hit him from behind. Claws raked his shoulder as he was sent sprawling to the ground. His broken arm hit a root protruding from the earth. Derec screamed involuntarily as the world went dim. His attacker, a wolf-creature, had turned to attack again, snarling. Derec tried to raise himself up with his good hand and could not. The wolf-creature gathered itself to pounce.

Derec knew he was going to die.

The wolf-creature, sentient or not, was going to rip his throat out.

Derec struggled to crawl, to move. He saw a blur of metal and heard the whine of overtaxed gears. Mandelbrot had moved to intercept the wolf-creature. But the gear-whine became a wail and the robot's leg seized up entirely. Mandelbrot started to fall, internal gyros protesting, as the wolf-creature leapt.

Mandelbrot's Avery-type arm snaked out even as he fell, even as the body of the wolf-creature bounded over the robot's prone body. Mandelbrot grabbed, held, and threw. It was all he could do. The wolf yelped in surprise and pain, then the body thudded against the tree next to Derec and slumped to the ground.

The stars in Derec's head went away slowly. His vision

cleared to see Mandelbrot lying next to him and staring. "Master Derec?" the robot asked. "I think I may have killed it." His voice seemed to grind from his metallic larynx, halting. Derec understood immediately that the robot was very near lockup. His one good eye was dim, and his hand was fisted tightly.

"Mandelbrot," he said desperately. "You had to do it. I would have died otherwise. I'm ... I'm okay, I think. You saved my life, Mandelbrot. You had no choice. No choice at all. If you lockup now, you're committing a First Law offense. I need you."

Derec tried to rise and fell back again with a groan. He'd intended it as an act—it wasn't. The pain was all too real.

His discomfort stirred Mandelbrot. The eye came back to full brilliance, the hand unclenched, and the robot stood up, his left leg sticking out stiffly in front of him. Gently, he helped Derec to his feet. "Thank you, Mandelbrot," Derec said and went to the wolf-creature. It was not breathing. Up close, it was magnificent: muscular, the thick fur rich with glossy highlights in the moonlight, the face expressive even in death. Derec's gaze was caught by the forepaws. They were true hands, despite the deadly curved claws, the long fingers delicate and jointed, the thumb opposed and ideal for grasping. The creature must walk on its knuckles, he realized, for the tops of those joints were wide, flat, and bony. Except for that difference, the hands might have been those of a human.

Derec sighed. Mandelbrot was right to be bothered by the death.

The massive head lolled, the neck broken. Derec stroked the fine, gray-tipped black fur of the creature with his good hand. "You couldn't help it, Mandelbrot," he said again, knowing the robot was watching him. "You have to know that."

He stopped. His fingers had found something in the fur of the creature's neck. Derec pulled it loose. It was a necklace of colored wire. Soldered to the end of one of the strands was a small circuit board. Derec's breath hissed in with surprise. "Mandelbrot, look at this! Mandelbrot?"

Mandelbrot was no longer listening. The robot had suddenly straightened in an attitude of listening. "Master Derec! The robots I heard a few minutes ago—they are being attacked!"

From somewhere very close by, they could hear the sudden, savage howling of wolves.

CHAPTER 19
ESCAPE FROM THE CITY

SilverSide's reaction to being seen by the Hunters was swift and powered by the Three Laws. The Third Law forced her to try to save herself. Second Law demanded that she follow the orders of humans, and though she was their leader, KeenEye's commands to save the kin still carried weight; the First Law compelled her to do whatever she could to keep her people alive.

Which meant the prime consideration was that Central be destroyed.

SilverSide changed her shape as the Hunters turned to look up at her. She drew back the parafoil and thickened the body. Even as the Hunters raised their hands to fire their lasers, she became a streamlined, compact mass instead of a glider, and she dropped the last thirty feet like a massive stone, crashing heavily into the central column of Central. Laser beams crisscrossed the air where she had been; delicate circuitry smashed under her fall. SilverSide changed back to wolf form even as she rose from the wreckage of the core unit. She went to the wide panels surrounding the core and pushed with all the strength of her durable body. A panel toppled, striking the next in line—the array went down like a row of dominoes, sparking and crashing, the thunder of their destruction ringing in the cavernous room.

SilverSide fled the room, howling the ritual triumph of a victor even as she anticipated the Hunters' lasers cutting her down. It didn't matter to her. She'd done what she'd come to do.

But nothing happened; the Hunters had stopped.

Already confusion was spreading through the city—she could hear it, a thousand voices crying out in the VoidTongue that the OldMother had given her. WalkingStones were asking Central for instructions, but Central was not replying, would never reply. The alarm was spreading out through the various levels of this *krajal*-like society.

EMERGENCY! Central core memory damaged and off-line Command program inactive: secondary routines down.

Activate supervisory backups.

Behind her, SilverSide heard the Hunters stir. She raced into the corridor beyond Central's room. There were no Walking-Stones in sight there. She quickly altered herself once more to appear as one of the Hill of Stars' Hunters, depending on the disguise to give her cover as she headed for the exit from the place. She listened to the continuing dialogue in her head.

City command given to Supervisor units Alpha, Beta, Gamma. The general announcement went out first over all frequencies, then three new voices boomed in her head. The direction finder in her skull indicated that all three were in widely scattered sections of the city.

ALPHA: Normal city subroutines accessed. City functions on-line and programming reinstated.

BETA: Alert situation! Central computer destroyed. Attacking unit in shape of local wolf-creatures is rogue robot. Repeat, attacking unit is robot not under control of City Supervisors.

GAMMA: Alert update. Witnessing units report sophisticated shape-changing abilities. Compass Tower Hunter-Seekers programming altered to compensate.

SilverSide increased her pace as she moved toward the exit. The corridor was crowded now, the WalkingStones returning to their routines. If the Hunters were aware that she could change shape, then her WalkingStone guise was not going to help her for very long. Someone would report her presence or discover the charade through some inadvertent response.

She knew that her victory had been short and bittersweet. Yes, she had destroyed Central. She had disrupted the city, if only momentarily. But the city had responded to the challenge all too well. If she interpreted the signals correctly, there were now three sub-Centrals, all in different places, and they knew her one advantage. If she were going to win this battle, she must move quickly, find all three of these Supervisors, and destroy them.

The next command from the trio of Supervisors dashed any hope SilverSide had at all.

ALPHA: All city units: access subroutine 3067.A.296. Immediately report any units not responding. Hold that unit at all costs until Hunter-Seekers arrive. Third Law precedence invoked—city survival involved: higher priority than individual survival.

All around her, moving WalkingStones came to an abrupt halt. An instant later, SilverSide did the same; it seemed safest.

She was wrong. A simultaneous alert was broadcast from the worker WalkingStones around her. *ANOMALY! Hunter-Seeker unit in Compass Tower has stopped.* In the same instant, all the workers in sight lunged for her.

SilverSide growled as she dropped back into her preferred wolf shape. She threw the nearest worker aside, the fragile body crumpling under her blow, and dashed through the opening it gave her. The alarm followed SilverSide as she darted from the building—she plowed through a worker who tried to block the entrance to the Hill of Stars and emerged into cool night.

She howled a lament.

Then she turned into the lumbering bird shape she had used once before, a black and sorrowing form.

Clumsily, her wings beat air, and she retreated from the city into the open sky. The false stars of the city below mocked her, and she knew there would be no hiding from the Hunters now.

CHAPTER 20
CONTACT

The uproar was furious, and mixed in with it was an occasional metallic grating, as if someone were bashing a steel plate over and over with a rubber hammer. All at once, there was a yelp of terror and a wail.

"The wolf-creatures," Derec said. "They're the ones who have been attacking the city. They're why we got the distress call. Look!" He held up the braided wire from the dead wolf-creature to Mandelbrot. It sparkled in the yellow-white light of the larger moon.

"The city does not know that they are sentient," Mandelbrot said. The robot seemed to shudder once all over. "The robots think they're just animals. They are simply exterminating them when they find them, like pests."

"This circuit board didn't come from the wolves originally. Sure, the city might think the wolf-creatures are just animals —after all, we did too. But they've obviously destroyed at least one robot already. Mandelbrot, we have to do something. Now."

Derec laid the necklace on the dead wolf-creature's body and took his gun in his hand, his face grim. Mandelbrot's hand closed over his wrist, firmly. "No," the robot said. The

106

odd grating slur was back in its voice. "I cannot allow you to kill them, Master Derec. I am sorry."

"Mandelbrot, you misunderstand."

"It does not matter if the robots are destroyed. That is only the Third Law and this Robot City can easily build more. I have made the decision you asked me about earlier. To kill a wolf-creature is to break the First Law."

"Please. You must trust me. I am not going to kill them." Derec tried to move his hand; the robot's grip was gentle but unyielding. "Mandelbrot, I am ordering you to release my hand. I will not kill the wolf-creatures. Do you understand that?"

Derec thought that Mandelbrot might not respond. The robot was staring at the dead wolf-creature, at the bright wire. The incident had further upset the positronic brain; Derec began to fear that Mandelbrot would freeze now, with Derec's one good arm locked in a death grip.

It would be an ignoble and curious way to end, anchored to a dead robot.

Mandelbrot's fingers opened slowly. Derec let out a breath he hadn't known he was holding. "Thank you," he said. "Mandelbrot, I'm going to need your help. I need a delicate touch and two good hands. Here—take the gun. Unload it. Quickly, we may only have a few minutes."

The battle was still going on within the darkness under the trees. In fact, the uproar seemed to have intensified. As the robot took the darts from their chambers, Derec opened his backpack and found the medical kit. Luckily, everything there was well padded and nothing had broken in his fall. He looked through the collection of vials, squinting in the dim light, and found what he needed.

"Mandelbrot, break open the dart chambers and empty out the nervekiller. Put this in."

"Master Derec—"

"It's a sedative. Undiluted, and with their body weight, it should knock them out."

Mandelbrot didn't move. His one good eye gleamed an unblinking, insistent red. "Master Derec, these creatures are unknown. Their metabolism might be so different from yours that this kills them."

"Or it may not work at all," Derec pointed out. He sighed. The sound of the nearby struggle was intensifying—he hoped there was still time. He patted Mandelbrot on the shoulder—the robot looked terrible: dinged, scratched, and battered. Having pieced the robot together from several different models and after the patchwork repairs following the crash, Derec felt pleased that the robot was still operating at all. He also hoped that he looked better, but the distorted reflection of himself in the robot's body looked just as disheveled and abused.

They needed help. Quickly.

"Mandelbrot, we can't communicate with them," Derec continued. "Twice now we've been attacked without provocation. They may be sentient, but they're also very dangerous. We need the robots. If we don't do something now, they may destroy all of them, and then they may well come looking for their friend here and take care of us."

"That is not certain."

"No, but it's probable. This is a chance that we *have* to take, one way or the other. A full-strength dose would take out a person of their general weight in two or three seconds and keep them down for an hour or two. Now—take the sedative and put it in the darts. I can't do it myself."

Derec held out the vial.

Mandelbrot hesitated, then the Avery arm extended toward Derec and its fingers closed around the vial. "Yes, Master Derec," Mandelbrot said. With delicate but quick precision, it began to do as ordered.

Mandelbrot reloaded the modified darts into the gun and handed it back to Derec. "Okay, let's go," Derec said. The shivering, challenging howls of the wolves still came from just behind the trees. Derec shouldered the backpack once more and began walking quickly in that direction. Mandelbrot followed more slowly, his left leg dragging and a distinct whine coming from his hip servomotors.

Derec broke through the trees at the top of a steep hill, the sides of which were bare dirt. Below, in a small, grassy glade well lit by the moons, a group of five wolf-creatures were struggling with four robots of the laborer type. One other wolf-creature lay dead from what looked to be a laser burn, but the robot fitted with the laser arm was already down—it was obvious that the wolf-creatures would eventually win this battle. They harried the robots, darting in with great leaps, ripping with the claws and tearing with their jaws, and then bounding away again before the robots could hold them.

As Derec watched, another of the robots slumped to the ground as a wolf-creature ripped a power connector away in a gush of violet sparks that left glowing afterimages in Derec's eyes. Mandelbrot was still struggling through the undergrowth toward him. The wolves were nearly two on one now, and Derec knew there was no time left if he wanted to save any of the robots.

He hoped this would work, but he knew that, though he couldn't say it, he was as skeptical as Mandelbrot. "The way things have gone so far. . ." he muttered under his breath.

He raised the gun, sighted down the long barrel, and pressed the trigger, aiming for a gray-furred male who seemed to be the leader. A *chuff* of compressed air: in the glade below, the wolf yelped and leaped into the air. On its hind legs, it reached around and plucked the dart from its skin, looked at it, and threw it down. The old wolf-creature's gaze swept around the glade.

It saw Derec even as he fired the gun once more, hitting another of the wolves.

The old one howled and pointed. Dropping down on all fours again, it charged. Derec counted softly as he fired three more times, injecting all the wolves. Another of them, unhindered by the robots, followed the old wolf's lead and—howling—rushed up the hill toward Derec. "One, two, three, four, five, six, seven . . ."

The wolves kept coming. They looked far more angry than sleepy, and Mandelbrot was still laboring through the trees.

"Oh, Frost," Derec hissed.

The wolf-creatures were fast and powerful. He knew he was not going to be able to retreat anywhere near fast enough.

He doubted seriously that he was going to be able to lose them in the darkness.

He threw the useless gun at the old one bounding up the hill.

It missed.

That figures, he thought.

CHAPTER 21

THE VOIDBEING

The old wolf-creature leaped over the edge of the hillside with the second close behind. The old one started to leap and then abruptly halted as if startled, pawing the ground with its clawed hands. The grizzled head cocked quizzically, and it growled something in its sibilant language.

But the younger wolf-creature following it had no hesitation at all. It flashed past the old one with a howl, baring its teeth and its claws flashing in mid-leap. Derec shouted and spun aside as the wolf hurtled toward him. It missed, through Derec felt the wind of its passage. The creature twisted in midair and spun as it hit the ground, kicking up dust. Derec waited for the creature to regain its balance and charge again.

There was nothing he could do. He was trapped between the old one, now snarling at him, and the younger attacker.

As Derec watched, trying to decide which way to run, the younger gathered itself again.

Whimpered.

And fell on its side. The old leader had fallen as well; down in the glade, the wolf-creatures had also been affected, dropping to the ground in the middle of the attack. Derec sunk down to the ground himself as Mandelbrot finally thrashed through the last trees. "Master Derec!" the robot called.

"I'm all right, Mandelbrot. It worked, I think." Derec gazed down in the glade below, glad that the nights were bright here.

The remaining three robots, suddenly free, had turned to take advantage of the situation. They advanced to the unconscious wolves, raised their hands to strike and kill—

"Stop!"

Derec's shout made them pause. They turned and looked. Derec stood at the edge of the slope, letting them see him fully. "You can see that I am a human," he said loudly. "You must obey me. Come here—the wolf-creatures are no danger now."

They stopped, though they didn't back away from the wolf-creatures. Mandelbrot came up to stand alongside him. "These creatures are no danger to me or to yourselves now," he repeated. "Come here."

"Yes, human master," one of them said. The trio headed for them as Derec and Mandelbrot examined the two sedated wolf-creatures beside them.

The drug had far less effect on the beasts than it would have had on Derec or any other human. Derec went to the leader; it was still awake, its disturbingly humanoid eyes watching him. The body twitched, muscles jerking without control as it struggled to rise and either attack or flee. Derec sat down beside it and stroked the head as he might have a dog. "I'm sorry," he said. "If we could understand each other . . ."

Mandelbrot was looking over Derec's shoulder. "It worked," Derec told the robot. "It wasn't what I expected, and I'm not sure how long it will last, but it worked. Now we need to get out of here before it wears off." Derec gave the grizzled lupine body a pat and laid the head down gently. The old one's eyes continued to follow his movements.

The three robots had reached them as Derec rose, slapping dirt from his pants. Derec tried to contact them via the chemfet link, but there was still nothing there but silence. "You're from the Robot City?" he asked them.

"Yes."

"Who is in charge there? Are there other humans? Is Avery there?"

"There are no other humans. The central computer directs all city activities."

Derec could feel his shoulders relaxing with their words, and he realized just how tense he'd been at the thought of another confrontation with his father and his twisted genius. He let out a deep sigh. "Then inform the central computer that you have found a human and will be returning with him and another robot to the city," he said. "Tell Central that we've come in response to its distress call, and that we have information for it regarding these wolf-creatures. Tell it also to open a channel to respond to Mandelbrot, the robot with me; I will communicate with the central computer through him."

The robots went silent for a moment, then one of them spoke again. "I am sorry, Master, but the central computer is not responding."

"Mandelbrot?"

"They are correct, Master Derec. There is silence on all . . . just a moment." Derec saw the other robots stiffen as if listening to something only they could hear; his own chemfet link seemed to be utterly dead. He could no longer hear the central computer at all.

"Master Derec," Mandelbrot said, "the situation in Robot City has changed radically. The central computer has just been destroyed by a rogue robot. The city is now under control of three Supervisor units. I have contacted them and informed them of your arrival and the situation here. They ask that we come to Robot City as quickly as possible for consultation. The robots here will guide us, and the Supervisors will send out more robots in our direction to escort us in case the rogue attacks us. It seems very violent."

Derec was puzzled. "Surely they don't think the rogue would attack a human, Mandelbrot? And how did the city ever lose control of it?"

"That is the odd thing, Master Derec," Mandelbrot answered. "It is *not* a city robot at all. It is not even humanoid."

Mandelbrot pointed to the drugged wolf-creature.

"It looks like one of these," the robot said.

The dark bird glided over the forest, silent except for the rushing of the wind past its widespread wings. Circling the glade once and seeing nothing, it banked sharply and descended, clipping the treetops and landing clumsily on the top of the hillside overlooking the clearing.

There, under the watching moons, it changed shape and became SilverSide once more.

The Hunters were still buried below. She noted that first of all because it was most important to her positronic mind—First Law. Three WalkingStones lay here as well, and that was also good.

But the dark shapes on the ground near the WalkingStones were kin. SilverSide howled a lament to the stars and then called for any of the other kin—there was no answer. She shifted her vision into the infrared and immediately saw warmth radiating from the ground nearby: two of the kin, and the shape of one was very familiar. SilverSide let out a glad BeastTalk cry and went to him.

LifeCrier was moving, at least. The old one had lifted himself up on his front legs and was trying to walk, though his rear legs dragged limply behind as if paralyzed. "SilverSide," LifeCrier barked in happy KinSpeech. "You've returned. Did you kill Central?"

"I destroyed it, but it did no good," SilverSide replied flatly. "What happened here? Are the others dead?"

"I don't think so." LifeCrier sank down again, exhausted, but his voice held a rich excitement. "SilverSide, there was a VoidBeing here. It had a companion, another WalkingStone unlike any of the ones around the Hill of Stars."

"A VoidBeing? From the OldMother?" LifeCrier's words stirred odd resonances deep in SilverSide's mind.

"Not from the OldMother. No, not with that shape. From another of the gods, perhaps. The VoidBeing carried a stick that threw small knives at the kin, and a magic in the knives took away our bodies while leaving our spirits inside. I attacked it because it had the look of the WalkingStones, and I knew it couldn't be from the OldMother. But before I reached it, I could no longer move. I could only watch as it came to me and touched me. I thought it would kill me then, but it didn't. It stroked me like a mother stroking her pup and talked to me in the VoidTongue even though it seemed to know I could not understand it. Then it laid me back down. It left a short time later with the WalkingStones from the city."

Delicate balances were shifting inside SilverSide. Core programming in her positronic mind gave her a feeling akin to yearning. She could hear the echo of the first voice she'd ever heard, talking to her in the VoidTongue in the darkness of the Egg. *A human being is an intelligent lifeform. A robot must obey the orders given it by human beings.*

But this VoidBeing is not of this world, she reminded herself, *not alive as we are. It is a MadeThing of the gods, or one of the gods themselves. So it cannot be human. The kin are human.*

The feeling receded, but only slightly. There was in her a pull toward intelligence. "I must go find this VoidBeing," she said to LifeCrier.

"It's gone back to the Hill of Stars," the old kin told her. "The WalkingStones went with it."

LifeCrier struggled to rise again and this time succeeded in standing on wobbly legs. The other kin were beginning to stir as well, easing SilverSide's First Law concerns.

Until she noticed that there was one less of the kin than there should have been. "Where is KeenEye?" she asked.

LifeCrier's grizzled forehead wrinkled. "I don't know," he answered. "We'd separated the kin to better fight the Walking-Stones, and she was to have attacked from over there." Life-Crier pointed into the woods behind them. "I never saw her." The others were coming up to them shakily, and LifeCrier asked all of them: "Did any of you see KeenEye during the fight?"

All the kin shook their heads.

SilverSide looked at the ground and the tracks left by the VoidBeing. It was an extremely clumsy creature; it had left a path through the trees that was as easy to follow as one of the WalkingStone's straight stone paths. An uneasy suspicion came to SilverSide. "Follow me," she said.

She ran into the cover of trees, LifeCrier and the others following slowly behind.

It took no skill at all to follow along the trail the VoidBeing had taken. The creature had broken branches underfoot and on all sides, and the ground still radiated the faint trace of heat from its passage. SilverSide saw a patch of kin-shaped warmth ahead and barked a quick hello.

"KeenEye!"

KeenEye didn't answer. The infrared red blotch didn't move. SilverSide took her vision back up into shorter wavelengths for detail, and then she saw the strange cant of the head and the odd way KeenEye was slumped on her side.

SilverSide growled, deep and warningly. She burst through the underbrush between them, hoping that KeenEye was simply sleeping as the others had been and knowing from the disquieting stillness that she wasn't.

"KeenEye?" SilverSide sat beside the body and lifted her into her arms. The head simply fell back, limp, the eyes open and unseeing; the neck was broken. SilverSide could smell the odd scent of the VoidBeing on KeenEye's fur along with the oily essence of the WalkingStones. That told her all she needed to know.

The VoidBeing had killed KeenEye.

SilverSide threw her own head back and howled her loss to LargeFace, singing KeenEye's spirit into the Void as she had seen the kin do with others who had died. From the trees, the kin—hearing SilverSide's sorrow—joined her with their own voices. The rising and falling of their song went on for long minutes, and then SilverSide let the empty body fall back to earth. It no longer held KeenEye; it was simply a dead husk.

"First we will return to PackHome," SilverSide said to LifeCrier. "And then I will come back here. If this VoidBeing lives in the WalkingStone's city, then it must be their leader."

She lifted her head and howled a BeastTalk challenge. "And if it is their leader, then it would kill all kin in the way it killed KeenEye. I must make sure that threat ends."

CHAPTER 22
BEST LAID PLANS

Derec had forgotten what a bath felt like.

"I have died and gone to heaven," he groaned as he sank back in the swirling warmth. Clouds of bubbles drifted over the enormous tub, and he lowered himself into the delicious heat until only his nose was out of the water. He could feel every bruised and aching muscle in his body starting to relax for the first time in days. Sitting up, he leaned back against the tiles, propping his broken arm (newly braced) on the edge. He motioned the attendant robot forward to scrub away the accumulated grime of his trek through this world.

Derec simply luxuriated, letting the robot do it all.

When it was over, he stepped out into the fluffiest, thirstiest towel he could imagine, allowed the robot to dry him, and put on a warm robe.

He felt soothed and comfortable as he went into the main room of the apartment.

The main room was as large and plush as the bathroom had been. Far up in one of the taller buildings of the city, immense windows on three sides offered a view of the sweeping expanse of the Compass Tower, by far the largest edifice in the city. Mandelbrot was standing there looking out at the landscape, along with another robot that Derec recognized as one of the Supervisor units. The antennae-studded globe of a witness robot hovered nearby.

"Master Derec, you look much better," Mandelbrot said, turning.

Derec grinned. "A bath does wonders, doesn't it. And I can certainly say the same for you." The dings and dents in Mandelbrot's body had been smoothed, his external linkages straightened, and his body polished. The robot's optical circuits now gleamed brightly, and when he moved, servos no longer protested.

"I am again fully operational," Mandelbrot said. "Master Derec, this is Supervisor Beta, one of the control units for this Robot City."

"Beta," Derec nodded. "There're a hundred or so questions I want to ask you."

"I can understand that, Master Derec," the supervisor answered. "Mandelbrot has told me of your journey here. First, I should tell you that the medbots who examined you tell me that you have no serious internal injuries. Your arm has been reset, and a drug that accelerates the knitting of bones has been given to you. Most of your injuries are bruises and contusions that will heal with time. You should be fully recovered within the week. As for your companion, Mandelbrot has been serviced and repaired entirely from parts in city stocks."

"For which we both thank you. But it's entirely possible that none of it would have been necessary in the first place had your central computer answered me."

Derec saw the distress his comment gave Beta; the robot's eyes dimmed briefly, and it backed away slightly. "You sent out a distress call," Derec continued, "but you wouldn't respond to our answer, either through contact via the original Robot City or via the chemfets in my body. Had you done that, we might never have needed to come here at all."

And Ariel and I might never have argued, he thought, and with the image of her that put in his mind, he felt again a deep sadness. *I have to call her. I have to apologize.*

"We deeply regret that, Master Derec," Beta was saying.

"Then why? It doesn't make any sense to ask for help and then ignore someone answering it."

Beta gave an oddly human shrug. "I agree with you, Master Derec. In explanation, all I can tell you is that this city was to be self-sufficient; there were instructions against direct contact with the original Robot City, but that does not explain why we would not respond to a human's inquiry. My fellow supervisors and I have conferred, and we assume the reason was a command in the central computer's programming. When the rogue destroyed the central computer, it also wrecked that portion of the backup units. None of the supervisors had been activated at that time; as you can see, the city is not very large or complex yet." Beta waved a glistening hand to the cluster of buildings below them. "There was no need to disperse city control. I cannot answer your question at this time, though we are attempting to reconstruct as much of the central computer's core memory as possible. If we learn more, I will inform you."

"It was Avery," Derec said with certainty. He rubbed at his damp hair with the towel. "He has the Key of Perihelion. He could have come here and programmed the central computer."

"That is possible. There is no way to be certain."

"Dr. Avery might still be in the city," Mandelbrot said to the supervisor. "In that case, Master Derec is still in danger."

Beta gestured to the window and the horizon, where the city nudged up against what looked to be an endless forest. "This city, as I said, is very small. I doubt that a human could be in the city and not be noticed."

"Your city let a rogue robot get in and destroy your central computer," Derec reminded Beta.

"The rogue has very special abilities," Beta answered. "We have taken steps to insure that it cannot do this kind of damage again. One of those steps was to activate myself and the two other supervisors so that city control no longer resides only in one place. And as you can see, a witness robot accompanies each of us, coded with instructions to return immediately to a haven should the supervisor be attacked. That way, very little of the city's knowledge would be lost should the rogue manage to destroy one of us. There are other supervisor units waiting to take over should that happen. We are also building new Hunter-Seeker units with special detection devices."

"Great, but I doubt it'll help much. I'd make you a bet that this rogue came from Avery," Derec said. "It has all his earmarks: inventive, cunning, and very, very dangerous. Which brings us to another problem. You've said that this rogue leads the wolf-creatures?"

"Yes. It was seen directing a pack of them that attacked workers on the edge of the city. They have given the city problems since the beginning, harassing our workers clearing the forest. As we felt them to be hindering our directives and to be dangerous both to ourselves and to any humans who would stay here, the Hunter-Seekers were directed to find and kill them."

Mandelbrot had swiveled to face Beta. "No," it said. "You cannot do that."

"I do not understand. All three of the Laws of Robotics demand it. By the Third Law, we must protect our own existence: they have damaged and destroyed units of this city. By the Second Law, we must obey the commands given to us by humans: they hinder us from following our basic programming. By the First Law, we must above all protect humans, and these creatures are undeniably dangerous. They attacked Master Derec and would have killed him had you not been there. How can there be any question about this?"

"Because it's not exactly that simple, Beta," Derec answered for Mandelbrot. "They're not just 'creatures' attacking you because you're here. I expect that they're protecting their home the same way I would. They're not just animals, Beta. They're sentient. They use tools; they have a language."

"Are you saying that they built the rogue?"

Derec sniffed. "Not a chance. They're barely at a Stone Age level. This rogue sounds more sophisticated than anything here."

"Then how did they get involved with the rogue?"

"I don't know that, but I'm willing to bet that Avery had a hand in it somewhere. The thing to do now is to figure out how to proceed without harming the wolf-creatures. There's a way to do that, I think."

"What do you want me to do?"

"The first thing that has to be done is to inform all city units to view the wolf-creatures as human. The First Law applies to them as well—you are to do nothing that does them harm. Will you do that?"

"You can do it yourself, Master Derec," Beta said. "We have reprogrammed the city to respond to the chemfets in your body. This Robot City is now under your direction. All you need do is give us your orders."

Derec had paid no attention to the chemfets, silent and useless so long. Now he opened his mind to the sub-miniature replicas of Robot City material. He could *hear* the city now, roaring in his blood. The flood of information was almost too much to comprehend, and he hastily closed down most of the channels, leaving open only the direct links to the supervisors.

You see, Master Derec? It was Beta, talking to him via the chemfets. *All Robot City is now yours.*

Good. Derec nodded and went to the window, looking out over the rooftops and up to the summit of the Compass Tower.

"Then we'll let the rogue in if it wants in," he said. "Avery didn't know that I would come here. Even a rogue has the Three Laws built into it. Avery might be able to design a robot capable of destroying other robots, but I find it hard to believe that even he could build a robot that could knowingly hurt a human."

SilverSide watched two of the cubs wrestling on the floor of PackHome. They rolled over and over on the dusty, broken stones, growling in high-pitched BeastTalk and nipping at each other with their sharp milkteeth. Finally one of them yelped in real pain and lay on his back, paws up and throat bared in submission.

It was ritual play modeled after the adults. SilverSide could hear one of the nursing mothers chuckling throatily as the victor gave a thin howl. She lunged and snapped at the triumphant pup from behind, and it screeched suddenly, leaping high into the air as the fur on its back ruffled in fright. The pup stumbled and fell, and the adults in the cavern laughed as it ran under SilverSide's legs for safety. The pup peered out at them half-puzzled, half-embarrassed.

SilverSide reached down and lifted it in her hands. "You see, the leader always has to be ready for a new challenger," she said to it in soft KinSpeech. She stroked the soft fur and set the pup down again.

The little one ran for its own mother.

"It's always good to see the younglings playing," LifeCrier said to SilverSide as the pup started to nurse. "It reminds you that even though our spirits leave here to go into the Void, OldMother will send them back again." LifeCrier licked SilverSide's face affectionately. "KeenEye will come back one day. She is not gone forever."

"I am not concerned with KeenEye," SilverSide said. "She is dead and doesn't matter any more." It was only true—there were no emotions in her positronic matrix, only the priorities built into it by the Three Laws. Yet SilverSide sensed that her uncaring words hurt LifeCrier, and she tried to explain to the gray-furred kin. "All that concerns me is how she died and why, and what I must do to stop that from happening again. You do not understand me, LifeCrier. You cannot see what is happening inside me."

They were all staring at her now: LifeCrier, the rest of the adult kin, the younglings. Their obvious respect and dependence on her stirred the boiling cauldron inside. SilverSide felt pulled in a dozen different directions at once. Things had seemed very clearcut and simple when she had hatched from the Egg. But now...

The part of her imprinted with the kin hated the VoidBeing who ruled the WalkingStones. Yet another part of her yearned to find this creature who seemed more advanced than the kin, who could fashion creatures from shiny stone and have them do its bidding.

LifeCrier had backed away a step in deference to SilverSide's rank. He lowered himself slightly to indicate subservience. "I don't understand KeenEye's death," he said. "The VoidBeing could have killed me or any of the others. Yet it didn't. I saw it raise its hands and stop the WalkingStones from hurting the kin it had paralyzed. It held my head and did nothing but stroke it. It did not seem dangerous."

"It killed KeenEye," SilverSide repeated. "I could smell its presence on her fur."

"I know. Still . . ."

"The WalkingStones seemed to obey it, you said. That would mean that the VoidBeing ranks higher than Central or these new Supervisors."

"I suppose. . . ."

"Then the VoidBeing must be an enemy of OldMother. It attacked you, even if it did not kill you. It saved the Walking-Stones and left with them. It had a WalkingStone as a companion. It is an *enemy*." SilverSide recited the facts in a monotone. Around her, the kin began to nod in agreement. Only LifeCrier seemed hesitant.

Inside SilverSide, synapses closed erratically. Her positronic mind no longer resembled that of any other robot; her life among the kin had changed it far more than her creator might have expected. In that sense, she was truly a rogue. No human standards worked for her anymore. She was an alien, and she had overlaid the Three Laws with an alien morality. She could not disobey them, but her vision of them was skewed.

"I must do what best protects us," she told LifeCrier. "Nothing has changed. We still cannot leave PackHome; my attempt to destroy Central only made it more difficult to damage the WalkingStones. You tell me that this VoidBeing is a being of flesh, and flesh is very fragile and very tasty. It had its knife-stick, but even a SharpFang has its teeth and claws. If the gods had to send it from the Void, then we must have hurt the WalkingStones more than we know. Perhaps if we also kill the VoidBeing, then the OldMother will have won. What do you think, LifeCrier?—you are the one who knows the OldMother best."

"SilverSide is the leader," LifeCrier answered, using Hunt-Tongue. "If she says that the OldMother wishes us to kill the VoidBeing, then we will kill it."

CHAPTER 23

STALKING THE GODS

Derec knew what the supervisor robot wanted before Gamma entered the room. The chemfets had told him, whispering into his mind.

"We're going to have to change your name," he told the robot. "Gamma—it shows a definite lack of imagination. But it can wait. What's up?"

"There are wolf-creatures on the far hill, Master Derec. They are approaching the city boundaries."

"I'm aware of it. They didn't give us much time, did they? Is everything ready?" There was little need to ask—he could have found out via the chemfets, but somehow it seemed more reassuring to ask the supervisor. There was only so much information he could absorb from the flood the chemfets allowed him. Even if he wanted to control every function of the city, it would have been impossible.

When the chemfets injected into him by his father had first asserted their presence, Derec had thought that he was going insane. He couldn't control them, couldn't handle the eternal input. But he'd learned how to filter out most of it, learned to let the city take care of itself. The supervisors were invaluable, and the lesson Derec had been taught in the original

Robot City was to delegate his authority. It was the only way to remain sane.

Derec yawned. He'd tried to sleep that afternoon, knowing the wolf-creatures would come at night, but he'd been too wound up. He yawned again, forcing oxygen into his lungs.

"Everything is set as you instructed, Master Derec." The supervisor robot, identical to its counterparts Alpha and Beta, went to the balcony high up in a building near the Compass Tower. City lights gleamed red and yellow on the robot's burnished skin. Mandelbrot came from the next room and went onto the balcony with Derec.

"I see them," Mandelbrot said. "There—just below the tree line. There are six or perhaps seven of them."

"Get your eyes fixed at last and you have to show off," Derec chided Mandelbrot jokingly, but the robot missed the humor entirely.

"I am sorry, Master Derec," he said. In retrospect, it was the only reaction Derec should have expected, but Derec suddenly knew how much he missed human company. *Ariel, especially. I need to talk to her. Sometimes I feel half-robot myself with the chemfets chattering away inside.*

There had been no time to contact her. Derec had known the wolf-creatures would come to the city again, and quickly. It was what Dr. Avery would have done, after all, and the rogue *had* to be Avery's—it just made sense.

He didn't think it would be much trouble dealing with it. In fact, his mood was rather jovial. Scrubbing away the filth of their journey through the forest and being in the city made him feel almost *human* again. He felt safe here, and with the resources of the city, nothing was impossible.

He'd be home again, soon. He'd see Ariel and patch up the rift caused by their fight.

The rogue was not a problem. The wolf-creatures he was more concerned about, but they should be easy enough, too. A general reprogramming of the city, an understanding of their language so they could communicate, and some compromise could be reached. This stupid war with the city would end.

Derec squinted into the night, cradling his sling in his good hand so that his injured arm wouldn't brush up against the railing. It was impossible for him to see anything at all. He couldn't even make out the individual trees, a kilometer and more away in the murk. The sky was overcast; even if this world's two moons had been up, their reflected light would never have penetrated the cloud cover.

"I told you they'd move," he said. "Can you see the rogue, Mandelbrot?"

"No, Master Derec, I do not. But it could still be there, back in the trees."

Derec shook his head. "No. Not that one, not if it's really the leader. If these beings are anything like the old wolves, they're pack animals. The leader would be first, or the others wouldn't follow. Remember Wolruf? Always headlong into the fray..." Derec grimaced. "I suppose it's possible it's already among the buildings, maybe in some other form. We might have missed it."

He shrugged. The city was alert now. The chemfets in his bloodstream fed him a continuous stream of information over the security channels. "Supervisor Gamma?"

"Yes?"

"You're certain the robots will consider the wolf-creatures human? You're certain they won't allow them to be harmed?"

"You have instructed them so yourself, Master Derec. If there were direct danger to you from one of them, I believe we would protect you first, as you most fit our programmed definition of 'human,' but otherwise, yes. We will not harm them."

"I can't stress that enough. The city can always build more robots. I don't care how many robots these wolf-creatures might destroy—I don't want them hurt. We can find some other way to coexist with them."

"That is understood, Master Derec. Mandelbrot has explained much to help us reinforce your orders."

Derec could feel adrenaline building inside him. He wanted to run back into the room and out to the edge of the city. He wanted to be there. He'd made plans to do so, but the idea had distressed Alpha, the supervisor to whom he'd first broached the subject. "That would be extremely dangerous," the robot had said, very slowly and carefully. "I do not know that the Laws would permit it. . . . The rogue robot . . ."

Derec could have argued; it hadn't seemed worth the trouble. Even Mandelbrot had agreed: the rogue was an unknown and obviously dangerous. Despite Derec's assurances that even a rogue would follow the Three Laws and thus be unable to harm him, all the robots had been noticeably "pleased" when he agreed to remain in the city. Okay. He'd play general this time, staying behind the lines and directing his forces. He noticed that the supervisors had also placed a cordon of Hunter-Seekers around his building, but he didn't comment on it.

"Give me the visual, Gamma. And make sure we're recording—we're going to need every scrap of sound these creatures make to start deciphering the language."

The wall of the building directly across from them was a milky white, translucent plastic. Now it glowed with inner light, and a huge image of the forest gleamed there, red with enhanced infrared imaging. Derec could easily see the wolf-creatures moving cautiously through the tall grass toward the city.

"Mandelbrot," he said, leaning forward slightly and pointing to the wolf in the front of the pack. "Isn't that the old one from the glade? See—it has the same gray fur around the muzzle, the same markings."

"I see him, Master Derec."

"He might be the best one to capture. He might remember that we didn't harm him last time. He might even cooperate. Gamma?"

"I have already so instructed all units, Master Derec."

"Good. I imagine we'll have to put most of them to sleep before they'll give up this attack. They seemed rather aggressive." Derec patted his arm and the bandages swaddling the claw wounds. He watched them moving slowly toward the city. "They're magnificent creatures in their own right," he said. "Look at them. So strong and sleek; we saw what they could do to a robot."

He could see now that several of them were wearing bright wire collars: totems against the city, perhaps, or simply trophies of past victories. The sight made him nod. "Mandelbrot, you were absolutely right. They *are* human. Maybe if Wolruf were here . . ."

As the pack approached, Derec sent messages through the chemfets. Several Hunter-Seekers advanced from the out-buildings of the city in a line. Half of them carried neural disruptors hastily built during the previous day: the computer models of the wolf-creatures indicated that the disruptors would interfere with the electrical impulses of the wolf-creatures' brains and cause mental confusion. The jury-rigged models had also been prone to leakage and had disabled more than one of the robots as well. As a backup, other Hunter-Seekers loaded with sedative darts also moved toward the invaders. Worker units waited to capture one or more of the creatures in hopes of learning to communicate with them.

Derec didn't think they'd go quietly. He fully expected a bitter battle before the wolf-creatures would be overcome.

He was wrong.

Halfway down the hill, the old one simply stopped. In full view, making no effort to hide himself, he rose up on his hind legs, pointed to the Hunter-Seekers, and howled in that eerie language. The gesticulation needed no translation—it was obvious enough: *Come and get me.*

There were evidently certain universals when it came to body language.

"That doesn't make any sense at all." Derec squinted at the meters-tall image of the wolf. "You'd think a pack animal would just attack."

"They are not just animals," Mandelbrot reminded Derec.

"Yeah. And I'll bet the rogue's taught them a few sneaky tricks of its own." He grimaced. "Well, he's obviously not going to come to us. Obviously they want the fight to come to them. Gamma, let's send the Hunter-Seekers forward."

But it was not a fight they wanted. Not at all. As the Hunter-Seekers advanced, the wolf-creatures retreated. Step by grudging step. They stayed out of range of the disruptors and the darts, though Derec suspected that was accident rather than anything else.

Derec tried direct communication through the Hunter-

Seekers, hoping they might understand the tone of his voice if not the words. They simply howled back at it.

He sent an unarmed worker forward, arms outstretched peacefully. When it reached the pack, they tore it apart.

At last, frustrated, he sent the Hunter-Seekers forward at a quick trot. The wolf-creatures melted back into the woods, and Derec called the Hunter-Seekers back.

As a confrontation, it was an elusive, aggravating thing. As an effort to solve the conflict, it was an utter failure.

"Frost," Derec muttered as the wall across the street went dark again and the city lights reasserted themselves. "Now just what in space was *that* intended to prove?"

SilverSide listened to the chorus of head-voices, waiting. She was just to the south of the city, having circled halfway around it from PackHome.

Already she could hear the alarm spreading as LifeCrier showed himself and the other kin at the edge of the forest to the west, and she could hear the new voice that directed the city functions, instructing even the triumvirate of Supervisors.

The GodBeing. The one of flesh, not stone.

The city was stupid. The WalkingStones had not learned. They expected the kin to attack the same way they always had, as if they could not create new tactics. She could hear the GodBeing telling the Hunters to move forward, speaking to them in the VoidTongue they both shared. *Do not kill them*, it said. *Capture the old one*.

SilverSide growled at that, pleased that she had cautioned LifeCrier only to show himself and to avoid an actual fight if he could. It was a First Law decision; SilverSide only knew that it felt right to her.

Do not harm the wolf-creatures. That was what the God-Being said, but SilverSide wasn't sure that she believed it. SilverSide could not lie herself—the OldMother had made such a thing impossible for her—but the kin could. *Flesh* could lie, and the GodBeing was flesh.

The city's attention was on the kin now. It was time for her to move.

She had tilted and canted the dodecahedral segments of her body so that they reflected as little light as possible. Becoming a WalkingStone had not worked the last time; she knew that the city was now aware of her abilities and would have taken precautions against that type of deception. Nor had the shape felt right to her.

Still, the Third Law demanded that she protect her own existence, and to enter the city as kin would have been dangerous. The bird shape had served her well twice now; she would use it once more until she found this GodBeing.

SilverSide's decision to accept the kin had given her a definite preference for their "human" shape. She *was* kin. She might enter the city as a bird, but she would meet this GodBeing as kin.

SilverSide willed her body to change. She spread wide, dark wings, and rose quietly toward the banked clouds.

The GodBeing would be near the Hill of Stars. She felt certain of that. The Hill of Stars was the heart of the city, and the GodBeing would be placed there, perhaps in the Hill itself, perhaps even in the room Central had used. SilverSide banked and swooped, letting the wind lift her as she moved toward the glowing pyramid in the center of the city.

Lights dimmed near the Hill, then a brightness glimmered on the side of one of the buildings. SilverSide brought her wings in, let herself drop lower as her optical circuits switched to a telephoto setting.

LifeCrier! She could see the kin, their images projected on a building alongside the Hill of Stars. In her head, the God-Being seemed puzzled by the kin's behavior, and it ordered the Hunters forward.

SilverSide circled the area, her eyes searching.

There! The GodBeing stood on a balcony opposite the view of LifeCrier, with two WalkingStones standing alongside it. SilverSide howled softly, banked, and plummeted like a stone as the wall showing LifeCrier went suddenly dark.

The wind whistled past her as she dropped in silence.

A few meters above them, she pulled up with a savage beating of wings. The WalkingStones noticed her at the same moment. SilverSide changed instantly into kin form and dropped. The WalkingStone nearest her she picked up and hurled over the edge of the balcony—it clutched at her desperately, missed, and fell with a strange silence. The other WalkingStone, an odd one with mismatched arms, immediately planted itself between SilverSide and the GodBeing. It made no move toward SilverSide, though she knew it would not let her pass.

The GodBeing was a strange creature, she thought, its face a pasty, dead color and its fur all gathered on the top of its head and nowhere else. It concealed its body behind some strange substance so that she could not even see its sex, and one arm was bound to its body. It had no claws, and its teeth seemed to be flat and dull like a planteater's. It smelled horrible, like some obscene cross between a dead WalkingStone and a TreeWalker.

It hardly looked formidable enough to be leading the WalkingStones.

And yet . . . SilverSide was strangely fascinated by the creature. It was a being of flesh, and it ruled this world of technology. *Find intelligence*, her old programming had ordered.

SilverSide shook the feeling aside. *Protect the kin*; that was what the First Law demanded.

"I challenge you!" SilverSide roared to the GodBeing in HuntTongue, but it only shook its head, not understanding. "I challenge you, GodBeing," she said again, using the VoidTongue. The words felt odd coming from her throat and yet were strangely familiar at the same time. The GodBeing reacted to her use of the VoidTongue, its eyes going wide and startled. "Let us fight to decide who controls the WalkingStones."

SilverSide growled and shifted into the challenge stance, her hind legs gathered as if to leap, her claws extended. The WalkingStone in front of the GodBeing began to move toward SilverSide, and she snorted. It reached for her, and her jaw clamped around its arm, tearing savagely. It was like chewing on stone, but the grasp gave her leverage and she flung the robot to one side.

The GodBeing backed away, trying to escape back inside the Hill of Stars, and SilverSide moved to block it. "No," she said. "I will not allow you to run. We must fight. That is the way to decide this."

"There is no need to fight," the GodBeing said. "You will not fight me. You will will aside from the doorway." There was a tone of imperious command in its voice. Almost, SilverSide wanted to obey, and for just a moment her stance changed, becoming servile and submissive. But she shook her massive head and growled again in angry BeastTalk.

"The OldMother sent me to save the kin. You kill them. We must fight. That is the way."

The GodBeing was shaking its pasty-fleshed head. "No. I've changed all that. I've told the city to stop. Back away now. You're a robot. You have to obey me."

"I am the leader of the kin. I obey the will of the Old-Mother."

"Who is the OldMother?" the GodBeing asked, and Silver-Side could not believe its stupidity. How could it not know the OldMother? Coming from the FirstBeast, it *must* know her.

But there was no time to question the GodBeing. From the edges of her peripheral vision, SilverSide caught movement; trebled movement. The WalkingStone she had flung aside was advancing toward her, and from inside the GodBeing's cave in the Hill of Stars, she could see two Hunters running toward the ledge and their confrontation.

SilverSide howled in fury and faced the GodBeing.

"You are afraid of me. I should be the leader. If you rule the city, then meet me. I will wait for you."

She flung aside the hand the WalkingStone laid on her and rushed to the edge of the ledge, knocking the GodBeing down in her leap. It was certainly a fragile being, for it cried out in pain as she plummeted over the side.

She willed herself to become the bird again and swooped up and away. The WalkingStones had helped the GodBeing to its feet and were watching her as she gained altitude. She watched them carefully to see if they aimed their awful fire at her, but the GodBeing held them back.

Howling her BeastTalk challenge once more, SilverSide left the city. Landing in the forest, she resumed her preferred form and sat down to wait.

CHAPTER 24

A CALL RECEIVED

It had to be one of the most frightening sounds he'd ever heard, those shivering howls coming from the throat of the huge black carrion bird. More than anything else, the fluidity of the rogue's body was terrifying. It had seemed to simply *melt* into its new shape. . . .

Watching the rogue fly away, Derec was suddenly very certain that this wasn't going to be as easy as he'd thought it would be. Not at all.

He took a deep breath of the cold night air. Cradling his arm, he went back inside.

"Master Derec, are you hurt?"

"Mostly my pride, Mandelbrot," he answered. "I suspect it'll heal slower than the rest of me."

Derec's arm was throbbing again, and his head ached where he'd hit the railing as the rogue swept past him, but none of it was as serious as it could have been. He'd seen those teeth, those claws, and he'd seen how the rogue had flung Mandelbrot aside like a broken doll. A few scrapes and bruises were nothing. Nothing at all.

Derec sat down on the couch and leaned his head back.

"We need Wolruf," he said. The city was still in an uproar.

He could hear it all in his head. Supervisor Alpha was directing the Hunter-Seekers to try to track the rogue, but Derec knew that it would be hopeless. There were too many shapes it could have taken to avoid pursuit.

"Wolruf?" Mandelbrot queried.

"Yes. Think about it. She'd understand these creatures better than we can. At the very least she'd be dealing with a canine intelligence that is—maybe—more like her own in contrast to our apish thought patterns. That's our problem. The rogue seems to believe it's one of them; their leader, in fact. Which means it's thinking like them. The rogue's logic is utterly alien. It's obvious that *I* didn't understand it," he added ruefully.

"It is still a positronic intelligence, Master Derec. It was built by a human, if not Dr. Avery himself. That much is certain. I observed it as closely as possible during the skirmish. The skin was definitely dianite, like the material of the city itself, and it spoke in Standard. There are certain givens with a positronic brain. It may even be that it will respond to the city's orders, being made from the same substance."

"Yes, Mandelbrot. It follows the Laws, or should, at any rate. I just wonder how it might *interpret* them. A pack society, a carnivore's mores . . ." Derec took a deep breath. "Frost, I'm thirsty." He went to a dispenser unit in the wall and ordered a drink, downing it all in one quick gulp.

"We can't understand these beings, not easily," he continued. "Wolruf has a closer affinity to them than we ever will. Besides, *you* were the one insisting that they should be treated as human. How can we do that if we don't understand them? How are we going to handle this rogue if we can't understand what it might be thinking?"

"I agree with you, Master Derec. Send for Wolruf."

"Good." Derec nodded. "It's about time I made a decent decision." *Which hasn't been since Aurora.*

Still holding the empty glass, he went out to the balcony again and stared out at the darkness into which the rogue had disappeared. The sound of the rogue's howling still seemed to echo. He felt the skin of his back prickling at the memory.

He didn't mention all the other reasons for wanting to

make the call, though he knew Mandelbrot would also be aware of them, if too concerned with causing a human pain to mention them. Wolruf's outlook would help them, yes, but Wolruf would also bring a ship which would allow them to leave the world if they needed to. And Derec wanted very badly to call Ariel. He wanted Ariel more than Wolruf in many ways.

Wolruf could also bring Ariel.

He sighed again.

Derec felt in his head for the chemfet channels and called: *Alpha. Beta. Status on Supervisor Gamma.*

Beta responded immediately. *Gamma unit inactive after fall. Positronic brain has been taken to repair station and will be reinstalled in a new body if possible. Extent of damage to brain is unknown; a new supervisor unit has been activated. Alpha reports that Hunter-Seekers have lost rogue. Instructions regarding rogue and wolf-creatures?*

You will continue to regard the wolf-creatures as human, Derec answered. *The rogue is not to be harmed if you do find it, but there's no need to send the Hunter-Seekers past the city boundaries. The rogue will be back.*

Derec was certain of that much.

Understood. Derec could almost imagine distaste in the flat, emotionless response.

In the meantime, I need access to the city hyperwave transmitters. You should have coordinates for Aurora in the city memory banks. Please transmit the following message:

Ariel: Find Wolruf. Send her immediately—imperative! And . . . I'm sorry. I love you. Please send an answer to these coordinates. And Ariel—I would like you to come with her. Derec.

The message arrived at Aurora as a highly compressed squirt emanating from the Aurora system's wormhole, punched through the incredible distances and the space-time anomaly by the powerful transmitters in Robot City.

The weakened signal was received by Aurora's orbiting communications complex, the charges billed against Ariel's family's account, and transferred down to the planetary net decoded and strengthened. There it was posted to Derec and Ariel's computer terminal.

That was exactly as Derec had intended, except that Ariel was no longer there to receive it.

Someone else was.

"Wolruf? Who or what is Wolruf? You must answer me. It is extremely important."

The household robot didn't seem inclined to answer the query. The inbuilt command against revealing an owner's business was perhaps the most highly stressed program code in its memory, the Second Law priority reinforced to the best of factory's technicians' abilities.

But there was one higher priority that could always be invoked, and the speaker was *very* skilled with positronic logic. The words simply had to be carefully chosen and constantly repeated.

"It is very important that you tell me, Balzac. Mistress Ariel is not on Aurora, as you know. She has left this world and cannot help. Master Derec is in trouble; that is implied by the message. He needs this Wolruf to aid him. *I* will contact Wolruf, but I first must know where to begin looking. You must tell me all that you know. This is a First Law situation, Balzac. First Law. Ariel and Derec are in danger, and your refusal to speak increases that danger. This supersedes any previous instructions you may have received. Do you understand?"

It took an hour of careful argument and resulted in a badly damaged robotic mind. Balzac would never be of much use to its owners again.

But it *did* speak, the words halting and slurred. . . .

CHAPTER 25
DECISIONS

For the next two days, Derec checked with the city communications center every hour or so, though he knew that he would have been alerted via chemfet if a message had been received.

There was never an answer. Ariel said nothing.

That was very unlike her. Derec was certain that even if she'd been furious, she would have sent back some scathing reply. But the hyperactive frequencies were silent coming from Aurora.

He hoped that she'd simply decide to head for the planet with Wolruf, that any day a ship would appear in orbit around the world. He instructed the city to turn its attention to the sky, to search the night for the faint glimmer of a ship's drive. Maybe she was out there already, a day or two away after the jump.

But the sky was devoid of ships. Derec waited for eight days, not eating or sleeping well and leaving control of the city entirely in the Supervisors' hands after giving them firm orders: *The city is to cease any new construction and any clearing of land. Remember that the wolf-creatures are to be regarded as human insofar as harming them. Do not destroy the rogue.*

As the days passed, the wolves grew less cautious. The

rogue appeared every night on the hillside outside the city, pacing the perimeter and howling in the speech of the wolf-creatures. Derec didn't need to know what it was saying; that was obvious enough. And the wolf-creatures seemed to realize that the city was doing nothing to resist them. On the third day after the rogue's challenge, the pack made a blitzkrieg attack on a party of workers, destroying most of them before the Hunter-Seekers arrived and the wolves fled. Following Derec's last orders, the Hunters didn't pursue the wolves but simply let them go back into the safety of the forest.

The rogue itself made a dash into the city on the fifth night, and it destroyed Delta, the replacement Supervisor for Gamma. The positronic brain was wrecked beyond repair; Gamma was restored to working status in a different body.

On the sixth night, a Hunter-Seeker managed to sneak up on the pack and sedate one of the wolves from a distance. But when two Hunters went to capture the creature, the rogue attacked from the shadows. The Hunter-Seekers were disabled; the rogue seemed unharmed.

It was apparent to Derec that the stalemate could not continue. It was also apparent that Wolruf, if she were coming at all, would not be there soon, and that Ariel had either never received the message or had ignored it and was not going to answer.

That left very little choice for Derec. He was entirely healed now, the broken arm knitted if still a little tender after the accelerated treatment. He had no excuses not to confront the problem directly. Anything was better than brooding.

Despite that, he was not at all pleased with the prospect.

Mandelbrot woke Derec from his sleep. "The rogue is outside the city again," the robot said softly. "I saw it in the distance, walking along the edge of the trees."

"Did you try ordering it in again?" Derec asked. With the help of the city's technical library, Mandelbrot had been trying to subvert the rogue's base programming, since it evidently had a comlink to the city. The robot had been broadcasting orders over various frequencies, but to no effect.

"Yes. In the Robot City program code once more and also

in human speech using a recording of your voice. It used the comlink to growl."

"Maybe you should offer it a biscuit," Derec grumbled.

"If you think that will work, Master Derec. One moment—"

Derec grimaced. The robot was already moving swiftly toward the door.

"No! Mandelbrot, come back here. Frost, can't you tell when a person's joking? Wait a second and let me get ready." Derec rolled out of his bed and rubbed at his eyes. "It's time I went to see it personally. It's time I answered the damned thing's challenge. The rogue's right; one of us has to be in control of things."

Mandelbrot's eyes glittered at him from the night darkness. Beyond the robot, the wide archway to the balcony was open. Neither of the moons was up; the sky beyond Mandelbrot's head was dusted with stars. The wolves would be out there now, and the rogue would be with them.

"Master Derec, I do not like this."

"I don't either, believe me." Derec pulled on his pants, tugged a loose-fitting tunic over his head.

"The rogue is dangerous. It has destroyed city robots, it has damaged the central computer, it has harmed the Supervisors. It has even threatened you."

"None of which necessarily violates the Three Laws," Derec pointed out. "Not even the threat. It's in the shape of those wolf-creatures; it thinks like them, too."

"In which case it is *very* dangerous. And I must disagree. No robot in a sane state could say what the rogue said to you on the balcony. Such a statement would cause extreme reactions within my positronic potentials. Even contemplating such an act now sets up vibrations that I can sense. To actually make such threats meaningfully would be impossible. The damage to my brain would cause an immediate dysfunction if not an outright freeze."

"The rogue follows the Laws," Derec insisted.

"The rogue is insane. It must be. Its interpretations of the Laws cannot be trusted. It injured you the first time you met."

"Nevertheless, I'm going to go meet it."

Mandelbrot stepped in front of Derec, blocking his path. "Master Derec, I cannot allow that. I am sorry. The First Law forbids it."

"This is a direct order, Mandelbrot, and I've already told you your assumptions are in error. This isn't a First Law matter. Step out of my way."

"I . . . am sorry." The robot's voice was slightly slurred, hesitant; the delicate balances between the Laws shifted, but it remained in place before the door.

"Mandelbrot, the rogue hasn't harmed me. Not really. It was protecting its own existence, and it made a judgment call that it could move past me. You might have made the same decision—a small bump against the likelihood of destruction. It *could* as easily have taken my head off with those claws."

"I . . . do not . . . know. . . ."

Derec saw that the robot's resolve was visibly weakening. He pressed his argument. "The rogue could have killed me in an instant, Mandelbrot. It chose not to. That tells me that the Three Laws are still functioning. And we're not going to resolve anything here unless we confront it. If we just order the city to build us a ship and leave—assuming the city's even capable of such a task at this point, and I seriously doubt that—then we've abandoned these wolf-creatures. They're going to continue to try to attack the city, and once we're gone, who knows what will happen? They may well die. We've certainly disrupted their society already, and if the city continues to grow, it will contact other packs as well. They're sentient beings, Mandelbrot. You know it yourself. I can't and won't just leave them, and just sitting here is useless."

As he spoke, Derec realized that he was also talking to himself. He *had* just been sitting there, moping about Ariel and Wolruf and doing nothing. It *was* time to confront the rogue, one way or the other. He had to face the challenge.

"Mandelbrot, I'm ordering you again to move."

The robot took a hesitant step aside. "I would like . . . to accompany you."

Derec smiled. "Of course. You always need a second in a duel." Then, before Mandelbrot could say anything else: "Just kidding, of course."

SilverSide watched the city as she'd watched it every night since SmallFace was a crescent horn. The moon was entirely gone now, waiting for the OldMother to birth it once more in its endless cycle. Still the GodBeing ignored her. But Silver-Side came every night and renewed her challenge.

The GodBeing would come to her. It must.

At least some of what it said had been true. The city *had* changed; it no longer pursued the kin when they attacked. Only a few nights past, LifeCrier had led the pack down to kill. Though the Hunters had come to protect the worker WalkingStones, they had not followed the pack when the kin retreated.

Then the youngling SlowPaw had been caught straggling as usual, and one of the Hunters had shot him. SilverSide had been certain that SlowPaw was dead. But the Hunters came after the body, and after SilverSide disabled them, she found that they had only made SlowPaw sleep. She had been certain that the Hunters would follow her for revenge and had been ready to lead them away from PackHome again.

But the rest of the Hunters remained in the city. The God-

Being—whose name was Derec, as she knew from listening to the city's VoidTongue—had ordered it so.

What kind of creature would stay hidden in its cave for so long? How could it hunt there, when all the game had been driven elsewhere? The GodBeing was flesh like the kin; it must eat.

Which meant that it would come out.

Most strangely of all, SilverSide could feel the urge in her to meet this GodBeing again. The remembrance of it stirred odd thoughts in her mind. She felt a pull, a yearning.

It has knowledge. It is intelligent. It is a toolmaker far superior to any of the kin. I have heard the city say that the one WalkingStone was built by this Derec.

There were moments when she did not want to fight it at all. But the challenge was demanded by the OldMother's commands inside her. Above all else, she could let no harm come to the kin, and the city harmed kin simply by its existence. She *must* control the city as she controlled the kin, and the GodBeing prevented that.

That meant it must be challenged. If it refused her that privilege, it must die.

The edge of the city was well defined, like the boundaries of a cooled lava flow. Derec stepped from a hard level walkway and with the next step, he was on grass. Outside.

He suddenly, foolishly, felt unprotected.

That's silly, he told himself. *Mandelbrot's alongside you, and Alpha's monitoring the whole thing through Witness robots. There are a half-dozen Hunters waiting back in the city; they'll get to you in seconds if anything happens. You're as safe as you can be. Besides, you're the one who insisted that the Three Laws protected you from the rogue.*

He suddenly didn't feel very confident at all.

A low rumbling came from his right. Derec turned.

The rogue was there.

It crouched fifty meters upslope where a stand of trees had been cleared by workers from the city. Perched atop one of the fallen logs and in wolf shape, the rogue looked bigger than

Derec had remembered. Its claws were displayed, its mouth slightly open to reveal the metal teeth set there. It reared up on its back legs as Derec turned to it, standing perhaps a half-meter taller than Derec himself. Mandelbrot had come alongside Derec without prompting, the implicit threat in the rogue's pose forcing the robot to stay close enough to intervene.

It's a robot. It follows the Laws. Derec took a deep breath, motioning Mandelbrot back. "I've come to talk with you," he said to the rogue.

It growled, then spat out in Standard: "I have challenged you already. I did not come to talk."

"At least tell me your name."

"I am called SilverSide," the rogue answered, and Derec could have sworn there was a hint of bravado in its voice, far more inflection than any robot he had ever heard before. Whoever had programmed it had been *good.* "I am the Chosen of the OldMother, the Bane of WalkingStones. Tell your WalkingStone to leave so that we may decide who is the leader."

Derec looked at Mandelbrot, who had taken yet another step closer at the rogue's words. "Mandelbrot is compelled to protect me, SilverSide. Tell him that you're not going to hurt me, and I can send him back."

"It is no protection to you at all," SilverSide answered, and her pale eyes glanced at Mandelbrot. "I have already defeated it once. I will do it again, and then you and I will settle this."

"No, I order you—" Derec began, but it was already too late.

The rogue moved faster than Derec thought possible. If Mandelbrot had not been there, Derec would not have had a chance. Derec felt a wind as Mandelbrot shot by him and met SilverSide.

The rogue collided with the onrushing Mandelbrot in a thunderous, resounding crash. There was a blur of violent motion, and Mandelbrot was suddenly down in the dirt, his legs thrashing helplessly from a severed cable held in the rogue's claws. The rogue itself had a long scratch in its flank but otherwise seemed unharmed.

Derec opened his mouth to shout, to protest, to scream. The chemfets told him that the Hunter-Seekers were coming, but they would be too late.

Much too late.

SilverSide growled terribly, flung the cable away, and was on him. He tried to raise his hands, hopelessly. Claws raked Derec's sides as she grappled him and bore him down. "No!" he screamed. "You can't hurt me! I'm a human—"

The rogue wailed.

"I'm a human—" the GodBeing Derec cried. The word set off a bewildering spark of reactions in SilverSide's mind. *Human!* The resonance from that VoidTongue word was stunning, and SilverSide reeled from its effects.

A human being is an intelligent life form.

Intelligence. Human.

"You are *not* human," SilverSide roared in denial, but she spoke in HuntTongue—the language of "humans"—and no answer came to her. Taking advantage of SilverSide's confusion, the GodBeing had rolled to its feet, and now she struck at it once more, intending to slash it open with her claws for its lie.

She could not. *Could* not. It was as if the OldMother controlled her hand and brought the claws back at the last instant so that she missed the GodBeing. She leapt at it instead, bearing it down again to roll it gasping in the dirt, then moving away a step so that it could stay on its back, submissive and beaten.

It either did not know to submit, or it would not. The GodBeing staggered up once more, defiant. SilverSide rushed at it again. The GodBeing screeched with pain as her arms wrapped around its chest and squeezed.

"Submit!" she whispered to it, and it was as if the Old-Mother's will made the words a plea. She wanted this to end. She wanted the GodBeing to go limp and end this farce.

She was so much stronger than this thing of flesh. The GodBeing was weak, weaker than the sickest of the kin. And yet it still struggled.

"No!" it shouted back, its face gone red, its eyes wide and

mouth gaping open. She could smell its breath, strangely sweet. "No. You must stop this. I order it. I am a human. You must obey me."

The words staggered SilverSide as if they were physical blows. Her grasp loosened, and the GodBeing sagged to the ground. SilverSide stared at it without seeing it, all her attention on the confusion within her.

Human.

You must obey.

SilverSide howled in BeastTalk.

Somehow, he wasn't dead. The rogue was howling again like a mad thing, and, as Derec stared at it, its body was changing. The snout was shortening, the ears moving lower on the body, and the canine jaws softening. Yes, the face was humanoid, and the features were startlingly like Derec's own.

"GodBeing, I . . . I must know . . . more," it said, and he could hear the confusion in its mind in its halting voice. Positronic drift. Derec began to feel some hope. "I . . . need information."

There was someone or something behind the rogue, some shape. Mandelbrot had managed to lock his legs and rise, lumbering stiff-legged to them and impelled by the First Law. Derec saw the blow coming a moment before it landed. "Mandelbrot, no—" he began to shout, but it was too late.

Mandelbrot's closed fist fell on the rogue's neck. It went to its knees, a wolfish snarl coming from its human mouth, and now it was changing again, returning to wolf form. "No, Mandelbrot!" Derec ordered again. "I'm in no danger!"

The rogue was confused. It looked from Mandelbrot to Derec, to the forest, to the Hunter-Seekers moving rapidly toward them. It screeched, a sound of raw animal fury, its features changing rapidly and ceaselessly. Human/wolf/human/wolf.

Wolf.

It stared at Derec. "Don't go," he began, but the rogue shook its head.

Dropping to all fours, it began to run for the cover of the forest.

"Come back!" Derec shouted. "I can teach you! In the city..."

But it was already gone.

CHAPTER 27
CHANGELING

Below, the kin huddled on the ledge before PackHome. The pups yelped and played mock fights and nursed. The younglings old enough to be in the Hunting Pack strutted and told fanciful tales about how they had helped SilverSide kill WalkingStones. The adults simply nodded and occasionally looked to the summit of the hill where SilverSide and Life-Crier had gone.

It had been a strange fight, that of SilverSide and the God-Being. They still did not know who had won.

"You are unhappy with me," SilverSide said in HuntTongue.

LifeCrier shook his grizzled muzzle from side to side. He used KinSpeech, telling SilverSide that she needn't be so concerned. "No, SilverSide. Not unhappy with you. I'm sad that you're leaving."

"I have not decided that. I have decided nothing."

"I can smell the change in you."

"LifeCrier has the nose of a DirtDigger," SilverSide said in HuntTongue, and LifeCrier bowed his head at the rebuke. He did not move away, though, standing his ground on the rise. They could see the Hill of Stars in the twilight, an aching

148

brightness, and they both stared at it for long minutes.

"I saw the OldMother move in you," LifeCrier said. "My eyes are not as sharp as KeenEye's, but you and the GodBeing . . ."

"I know. I felt it."

"What will you do?"

SilverSide howled, and after a second, LifeCrier joined her. Their twined voices caused flocks of birds to rise in the trees below. "I am kin," SilverSide said at last. "I lead the litter-kin here."

"I know. No one would challenge you. You are the Old-Mother's Gift."

"I am kin," SilverSide repeated. "Yet . . ." She stopped and looked at LifeCrier.

"I must do what is best for kin," she said.

LifeCrier nodded. "That is all the OldMother would ever ask," he told her.

"Derec!" Mandelbrot whispered urgently and pointed.

Campfire and city lights glinted on the robot's polished body; the red gleam of its eyes glanced at Derec and then back into the night darkness beyond the city.

Derec rubbed sleep from his eyes. He struggled from under his thermal blanket and stood. The night was very quiet. Even the brilliantly lit city at his back seemed quiet, though he knew that thousands of robots were about their tasks there. The sweet odor of woodsmoke filled the air; a gentle and cool night wind tossed the mane of smoke back toward the city.

They'd been camped outside the city for the past two nights, waiting. Each night he'd expected the rogue to come to him. The city was broadcasting an endless invitation to SilverSide. *Come into the city. You will not be harmed. The city's library is open to you. Come and learn.*

At last, it looked like it would answer the invitation.

The only question was *how.*

On the wooded crest of a hill, Derec saw the wolf-creatures. Their dark, quick shapes moved like fleet shadows under the swaying rooftop of the trees. Both moons were up; despite the city's glare and the campfire, Derec could see them quite well. Mandelbrot had moved near Derec, ready to protect him should the wolf-creatures show any hostility.

Hunter-Seekers can be sent, Alpha reminded him.

No. Not yet, anyway.

The shivering howls and barks of the wolf-creature's language drifted down toward them. Derec shuddered. In the weeks he'd been on this world, he still hadn't become used to that sound. Mandelbrot noticed and shuffled even closer. "Old racial memories die hard," he told the robot.

"The rogue is with them," Mandelbrot said. "They're gathering around it. Master Derec, I think we should have the city call the Hunter-Seekers. I am not sufficient protection for you. Regardless of whether the rogue will harm you, the wolf-creatures are certainly not bound by the Laws. . . ."

"I've already ordered Alpha to hold them back, Mandelbrot. The wolves are no danger. Not yet. Be patient; you're the one who worked so hard to convince me they're intelligent, remember?"

"Intelligent is not a synonym for 'not dangerous,' " Mandelbrot pointed out. "You as a human should be well aware of that."

"*Hmph.*" Derec snorted. "We'll wait, anyway."

The pack had gathered at the edge of the trees closest to the city. Derec could see the rogue now, glinting in the moonlight between the pacing outriders of the wolf-creatures. Now it stepped out into full moonlight, the old one at its side. The two licked each other, nuzzling and giving playful nips. Then the rogue began walking alone down the grassy slope toward Derec and Mandelbrot.

Halfway down, the robot turned and looked back to the pack, which had gathered at the lip of the hill to watch the descent. The rogue lifted its muzzle to the wolves and gave a long, ululating lament.

The wolves chorused back.

To Derec, they sounded wild and sad.

The rogue began picking its way among the rocks toward Derec's camp once more. As it approached, the rogue's body began a slow metamorphosis. *Step*—the lupine muzzle shortened; *step*—the tail began to shorten and retract into the body; *step*—it raised up to walk on its hind legs; *step*—and the legs themselves altered, the knees beginning to flex forward.

When the robot stopped a few meters in front of them, it was recognizably humanoid in the firelight. It glanced at Mandelbrot, then at Derec.

"GodBeing Derec, I have come to learn," it said. Except for the stilted, formal grammar, its voice sounded very much like Derec's. "I have come so you may teach me of the Void from which we both fell. I have come to learn what is human."

Derec nodded. He pointed back to the city and the looming bright presence of the compass Tower. "The answers are all in there," he said. "Follow me, and I'll show you the way. Mandelbrot, if you'll take care of the fire, please . . . we wouldn't want the woods to burn." He said it mostly for the rogue's benefit, wanting it to understand that he was concerned about the well-being of the wolf-creatures.

It was difficult for Derec to give the rogue his back. He half expected it to leap on him again, biting and tearing. He listened intently for a suspicious sound behind him. Derec knew that Mandelbrot was already on edge and would respond instantly, but still . . .

Nothing happened.

Alpha, we're coming in. The rogue is with me.

We will have the apartment ready, Master Derec.

Derec began walking, then glanced back when he didn't hear the robot following. It was staring back at the forest, and as it did, the malleable face went vaguely wolfish again.

"It's your choice," Derec told it softly. "I won't force you to make that decision. Come with me or go back to them. I won't try to stop you."

The robot howled to the wolves one last time, the bestial sound eerie and wrong to be coming from that human-shaped throat.

Then the rogue turned from the darkness of the trees and the huddled pack.

It followed Derec into the eternal light of the city.

Illustrations by Paul Rivoche

DEREC: An amnesiac who awakens inside a Massey survival pod, marooned on an asteroid composed of ice, his past and identity are total mysteries to him. Despite his amnesia, his intelligence remains unaffected, and he knows a great deal about robotics. He has adopted the name found on his clothing, apparently the name of the manufacturer.

DATA BANK

Illustrations by Paul Rivoche

KATHERINE ARIEL BURGESS, "KATE": Kate is a native Auroran, banished from her homeworld because of an incurable disease. Despite her illness and a pampered upbringing, Kate is headstrong, tough, demanding, and resourceful. On the advice of the medical robot Galen, she refuses to tell Derec what she knows of his past life.

WOLRUF: This caninoid alien, of roughly human intelligence, became Derec's friend when he was a prisoner of the pirate Aranimas. Although she served as Aranimas's aide-de-camp, she was an indentured servant, and she and Derec worked together to free themselves. When Derec and Ariel first went to Robot City with the Key to Perihelion, Wolruf and the robot Mandelbrot contrived to follow them. It was she who first raised the question for the Robot City robots of whether an intelligent alien should be obeyed under the First Law.

LIFECRIER: His name is also a title. LifeCrier is the eldest of the litter-kin SilverSide encountered, and his predecessor held the same name. The history of the kin is entirely an oral tradition, for they have no written language at all. The entire repository of tales, anecdotes, information, and mythology is given by a LifeCrier to his or her chosen successor.

LifeCrier's duties to the kin are many. He is charged with educating the young; he holds the past history of the kin and adds new events to the chronicle; he remembers the lineage of each member of his pack (matriarchal in the case of the kin, since the females mate with more than one male); he interprets celestial and worldly events in terms of their religious significance.

LifeCrier is priest, chief elder, head teacher, technical resource, and librarian for the tribe. In this, LifeCrier's role is perhaps even more important than that of the actual leader of the kin.

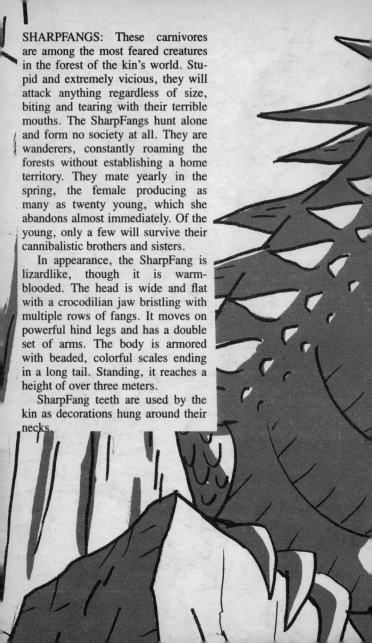

SHARPFANGS: These carnivores are among the most feared creatures in the forest of the kin's world. Stupid and extremely vicious, they will attack anything regardless of size, biting and tearing with their terrible mouths. The SharpFangs hunt alone and form no society at all. They are wanderers, constantly roaming the forests without establishing a home territory. They mate yearly in the spring, the female producing as many as twenty young, which she abandons almost immediately. Of the young, only a few will survive their cannibalistic brothers and sisters.

In appearance, the SharpFang is lizardlike, though it is warm-blooded. The head is wide and flat with a crocodilian jaw bristling with multiple rows of fangs. It moves on powerful hind legs and has a double set of arms. The body is armored with beaded, colorful scales ending in a long tail. Standing, it reaches a height of over three meters.

SharpFang teeth are used by the kin as decorations hung around their necks.

THE CENTRAL COMPUTER: In its earliest stages, all functions of a Robot City are overseen by the central computer (or "Central"), often housed in the Compass Tower of the city. Central is built by the first workers upon arrival on a new world. The computer quickly takes control of the city's rapid expansion.

The core programming is contained here as well as the city's main memory banks. While positronic in nature, Central is essentially a supercomputer rather than a mobile robot unit. Like all positronic intelligences, Central uses a platinum-iridium "sponge" to mimic the complexity of a human brain, and an array of chip-studded panels serve as its vast memory of files.

As a Robot City grows in size, control is eventually passed to several Supervisor robots, which allows for redundancy in the system as well as efficient specialization of duties. Central will still continue to function as the main source of city information as well as a competent backup in the unlikely event that all supervisor units should fail.

THE UNFORMED ROBOT: This is an experiment in positronic logic and capabilities conducted by Janet Anastasi, the mother of Derec and once the wife of Dr. Avery. Anastasi is a robotics engineer without peer, perhaps even more innovative than her former husband. In fact, it was his jealousy of her abilities that caused the first rifts in their relationship.

Her newest robot was programmed with the Three Laws but given very little definition or instruction beyond that. It was to find the most intelligent life on the world in which it found itself, and to consider that lifeform human.

Constructed of dianite, an advanced form of the substance of Robot City itself, the robot is infinitely malleable, able to conform to whatever shape "humankind"

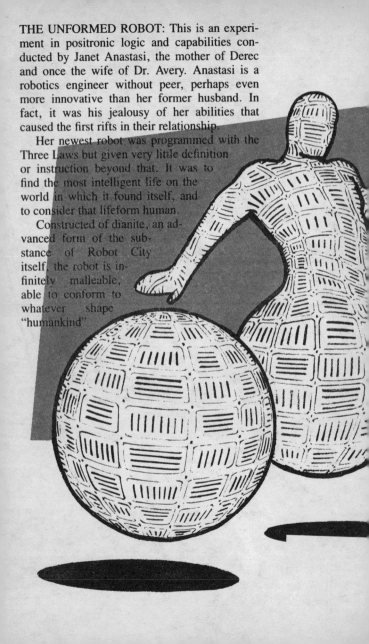

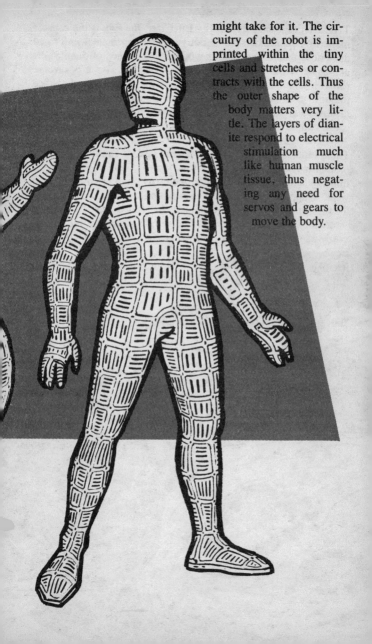

might take for it. The circuitry of the robot is imprinted within the tiny cells and stretches or contracts with the cells. Thus the outer shape of the body matters very little. The layers of dianite respond to electrical stimulation much like human muscle tissue, thus negating any need for servos and gears to move the body.

THE EGG: Aptly dubbed by LifeCrier, the Egg is the capsule used by Janet Anastasi to deliver her experimental unformed robot to the surface of this world. Also formed of dianite, the capsule is not simply a delivery device but also a positronic robot of very limited intelligence. Roughly spherical (hence LifeCrier's name) and solid-rocket propelled, the capsule has moveable, stubby wing surfaces and probe sensors so that it can choose a viable landing site and maneuver there.

The unformed robot sits inside a gel-filled compartment that protects it from both the intense heat of atmospheric entry and the jarring impact of the touchdown. Upon impact, the gel is evacuated, and the capsule begins its scant programming of the neophyte robot inside via a neural net. Once these carefully chosen bits of information are coded into the robot's memory, the capsule opens. The neophyte is then free to follow its first and primary instruction: *Serve intelligent life*.

STEPHEN LEIGH

Stephen Leigh is the author of several science fiction novels, including *Crystal Memory*, *The Bones of God*, the *Neweden* trilogy, and the first book in the *Dr. Bones* series. He is also a contributing author to the Hugo-nominated *Wild Cards* shared world anthologies, and has had several pieces of short fiction in such markets as *Analog*, *Isaac Asimov's Science Fiction Magazine*, and various anthologies. His current project is an off-beat contemporary fantasy novel entitled *The Abraxas Marvel Circus*. He is married to Denise Parsley Leigh; they have two children, Megen and Devon. He is also employed by Kelly Services as an Office Automation Manager. Other interests include Aikido, juggling, working with his Macintosh, and finding spare bits of free time.

WELCOME TO
ISAAC ASIMOV'S

ROBOT CITY ™

A wondrous world of robots opened up for the first time to today's most talented science fiction writers. Each author takes on the challenge of wrestling with the mystery of Robot City. Laden with traps and dazzling adventure, each book in the series integrates Asimov's "Laws of Humanics" with his famous "Laws of Robotics."

___ Book 1: ODYSSEY Michael P. Kube-McDowell   0-441-73122-8/$3.50
___ Book 2: SUSPICION Mike McQuay   0-441-73126-0/$3.50
___ Book 3: CYBORG William F. Wu   0-441-37383-6/$3.50
___ Book 4: PRODIGY Arthur Byron Cover   0-441-37384-4/$2.95
___ Book 5: REFUGE Rob Chilson   0-441-37385-2/$2.95
___ Book 6: PERIHELION William F. Wu   0-441-37388-7/$3.50

COMING SOON

ROBOT CITY BOOKS 7-12

© Byron Preiss Visual Publications, Inc.